Book Four in the Nestled Hollow Romance series

Copyright © 2019, 2023 by Meg Easton

Cover Illustration by Covers and Cupcakes

Interior Design by Mountain Heights Publishing

Author website: www.megeaston.com

"Sweet romance at its best!
I want to visit Nestled Hollow over and over again!"

-Elana Johnson
USA Today bestselling author of the *Hawthorn Harbor*
series and the *Getaway Bay* series

"Romance done right!
This series is going to be a keeper!"

-Kimberly Krey
Best-selling author of the *Sweet Montana Brides* series

more than friends in the
middle of main street

more than friends in the middle of main street

A NESTLED HOLLOW ROMANCE

MEG EASTON

contents

one

COLE

Cole hadn't gotten away from the restaurant as early as he had scheduled, and he'd been behind all night. He'd even gotten his daughter, Samantha, tucked into bed a full fifteen minutes late.

But even though it had taken all evening to catch up, here he was at 10:30, getting into bed at exactly the time he should be. It felt good to at least end the day on schedule, especially after being off so much of the day.

He picked up the book he was reading on how to raise a confident tween and had only gotten through two pages when a text lit up his phone. It was from his best friend, Brooke. He slid to open the text.

> Brooke: Mrs. Holt texted that you've got a bear in your yard that you should probably scare off.

> Brooke: She can see it from her bedroom window.

His brow crinkled. *Strange.* He typed back a message and touched send.

> Cole: Why did she text you about it?

> Brooke: She said, and I quote "That boy keeps such an exact schedule, he was probably in bed by ten, and I just didn't want to wake him up."

He shook his head. There was nothing wrong with keeping to a schedule— doctors recommended it for the best sleep— but even with a tight schedule, a bear in his yard was a good enough reason to text a neighbor after you thought they might be in bed. He got up and put his bathrobe on over his pajamas so he wouldn't freeze in the chilly night air, and texted Brooke back.

> Cole: So she texted someone in New York instead?

> Brooke: She didn't know I was out of town.

Brooke: Your bedtime is 10:30, and you read for exactly 12 minutes before calling it a night. It's only 10:37, so I know you didn't already fall asleep.

Brooke: You should probably go check on that bear.

Cole: I've got my bathrobe on, flashlight in hand, almost to the door. If I don't text back in 5 minutes, assume I got mauled by the bear.

Cole had heard of bears coming down from the mountains and rifling through people's trash, but not for a long time, and rarely in Nestled Hollow. Hopefully, Mrs. Holt just saw a big dog or something, and not an actual bear.

He flipped the flashlight on, opened the front door, and listened for a moment, shining the flashlight around the front yard. When he didn't hear any sounds or see anything suspicious, he crept toward the side of his house nearest Mrs. Holt's, sweeping the flashlight back and forth, looking for any movement, every sense on alert to danger.

The sideyard was empty of large, potentially lethal animals, so he crept toward the back of his house. He was just passing some of his taller shrubs when movement from the corner of his eye caught his attention, then something leaped out of the shrubs, roaring.

Cole yelped, jumped back, and dropped his flashlight before he realized what he was seeing. "Brooke! What are you doing here?" He picked up the flashlight and shone it in her direction, trying to see her without it blinding her, before aiming it at the ground. "You nearly gave me a heart attack. Aren't you supposed to be in New York until tomorrow?" He tried to slow his breathing and his racing heart.

Brooke attempted to stifle her laughter. "I caught an earlier flight and drove into town moments ago. That look on your face was priceless. I wish I would've recorded it."

"But what are you doing *here*, in my shrubs?"

"You mean besides admiring your bathrobe?"

Cole chuckled and shook his head. They'd been friends for long enough that she couldn't make him embarrassed by something as small as being seen in his pajamas.

"I came to bring you this."

Brooke held out the bear, and Cole shone his flashlight on the small stuffed animal. He read the words on the little guy's shirt out loud. "'Being away from you is unBEARable.' Aww, that's sweet."

Being out here, standing against a backdrop of stars, the moonlight bathing her face in silver light, her expression earnest and open and full of mischief, Brooke was breathtaking. Her eyes sparkled, her flawless skin shone, and her full lips, curved into a smile, making his heart rate pick up again.

And even though she'd spent the last half a dozen hours traveling, she still smelled as intoxicating as always. He didn't know what kind of perfume she wore, and couldn't pick out what the individual scents were, exactly. All he knew was that it was bold, yet soft, radiant, and completely captivating. A smell that was exactly, perfectly Brooke.

He shook his head. This was another reason why he shouldn't be out after bedtime. It weakened his normally strong ability to resist Brooke. That ability had only weakened to dangerous levels once, four months ago, and he vowed to never let it again.

It was late on a Friday night, and they were cleaning up the mess of paper snips left from the snowflakes they had been cutting out with Sam before he had gotten her to bed. He and Brooke had kissed, and it had been glorious and amazing for about the four seconds it took for Cole's brain to kick in and stop it.

He had told her, "I'm sorry. I can't do this to Samantha. I know how you feel about marriage and commitment, and I can't compromise with my kid on the line."

Their friendship had only recently recovered from the awkwardness and gotten back to feeling normal and easy again. Even still, though, he tried to limit the time he spent with her because it was just too risky. His heart was on the line, too, so he just needed to keep the mindset that they were nothing more than friends, and that's all they ever would be.

"I got one for Sam, too." Brooke pulled a little stuffed cat from her bag and held it out to Cole. It was wearing a shirt that said, "Stick with me. I'll leave you FELINE good."

Cole took the cat, tried to ignore the feel of her soft skin against his as their hands brushed, and said, "Sam will love this."

"I know. Now race me around your house. First one back to the bear sighting wins."

"Race you...around my house?"

Brooke nodded.

"Brooke, it's late. It's dark. And we should both probably be in bed."

"Because now it's after ten forty-two? I'll tell you what. I've been gone for five days— you name one time you've been spontaneous in the past five days, and we'll call the race off."

"Define 'spontaneous.'"

"*Choosing* to do something that wasn't on your schedule for the day."

Cole opened his mouth to say something, but no words came out, so he closed it. Then he said, "I'm both parents for Sam. If I don't schedule everything, things will fall through the cracks."

She ignored his protest. "Ready?"

"Exercise right before bed causes insomnia," Cole said.

"Nah. It just makes you good and tired so you'll fall asleep quickly. Set?" Brooke crouched down into a racing position.

If it had been anyone else at his house this late on a weeknight, trying to get him to race around the house, he'd have already been back inside by now. Brooke just had a way of convincing him to do crazy things he'd never do otherwise. "I've got longer legs, so you won't be able to win." He was still vocally protesting but found himself getting in a position to take off running anyway.

"And I had a coffee mid-flight to keep from being drowsy on the drive from the airport, so *you* won't be able to win. Go!"

Brooke took off running, and Cole raced after her a moment later. She leaped over the two-and-a-half-foot high fence into the backyard, so he did the same. She darted around the swing set, but he ran right between two swings and caught up to her as she ran right through the sandbox. They were neck and neck as they reached the fence to the sideyard, and they leaped almost simultaneously. Brooke stumbled a bit as she dodged the garbage cans against the side of the house that had been hiding in the shadow of the moon, but she grabbed the arm of his bathrobe and pulled it backward.

He'd learned long ago that she was in it to win and that she enjoyed some good competition. So he slipped his arms out of the bathrobe as he ran, leaving it in her hand, and made it to the front yard before her. Brooke cut across the porch, though, and leaped over the railing at the other end, landing at the side yard. They reached the starting point at almost exactly the same time.

A smile spread across Cole's face as he stood in his t-shirt and pajama pants, breathing heavily, feeling exhilarated and refreshed after such a rough day. Brooke seemed to have a way of knowing exactly what he most needed and talking him into doing it, even if he hadn't realized how much he needed it. "It's good to have you back in town, Brooke."

Brooke pushed the bathrobe into Cole's chest and he grabbed hold with the hands that still held the stuffed animals she'd brought. "It's good to be back." She put her hand on his shoulder. "Now that I've worn you out, you should be able to sleep like a baby. And I'll sleep better knowing that you're not dying from spontaneity deprivation."

His shoulder muscles involuntarily flexed at her touch, but he didn't allow himself to think about how it felt to have her hand rest there.

"Thanks for having my back," Cole called out as Brooke walked toward her car, and she turned and waved.

He stayed outside until she pulled away and drove down the street toward her house. It didn't matter how attracted he was to Brooke or how long ago he'd fallen for her— for his daughter's sake, he would never have a future with Brooke.

two

BROOKE

Early the next morning, Brooke stood at her design table in the back rooms of Best Dressed, sketching a new dress design. On the airplane the previous night, she had sat next to a fascinating woman and, as usually happened when she was talking with someone, the perfect dress for them came to mind.

The fifty-something-year-old woman was a humanities professor and, in her younger years, a CIA field agent. She still had the hints of strong lines and angles from her earlier years but had been softened by age, experience, and a kindness that shone on her face.

The business dress Brooke was sketching had the same feel. Strong lines that showed off the woman's regal presence, but softened. A dress that would look powerful on stage while giving a keynote address at a conference, yet perfectly at home offstage cradling a grandbaby.

Her brand, *By the Brooke*, wasn't a collection meant for one specific type of person. They were meant to show all the strong, diverse personalities of the human race. She loved when someone inspired a project that would represent a portion of the population that had been missing from her collection.

She stifled a yawn. The late coffee may have been a mistake. Or possibly the race around Cole's house. Or maybe the mix of the two.

Whatever it was, she was paying for it now. She had been wired when she had finally gotten home, so she couldn't fall asleep and couldn't stop thinking about the dress. When she finally did fall asleep, she even dreamed about it. She probably should've been working on other business stuff after being away, but she wasn't going to stop dreaming about it until her sketches were complete.

As her two employees, Noemi and Delbrina, unlocked the back door and walked in, chatting, Brooke looked up and smiled.

"Brooke!" Noemi said as she ran in and hugged her. "I thought your plane didn't come in until this afternoon!"

"I finished early and there was a flight with a seat available last night, so I got home about eleven."

"Yet you still beat us into work, while we're slower than a Sunday afternoon," Delbrina said as she hung her purse and jacket on its hook and pulled a stool up to the design table. "Ooo, that's beautiful. Are we going to test this dress in my size?"

Brooke laughed. Whenever she designed anything with strong lines and angles, Delbrina wanted to test it. Anything flowing and girly, Noemi wanted to try. "I wouldn't have it any other way." She slipped the paper into her design portfolio. "We've got a lot to get done today. Are you two ready for our team meeting?"

Noemi joined them at the design table. "Only if it starts with you telling us how your meeting with Van Zandt Corporate went."

They *did* have a lot to do today, especially since she'd been gone. But Brooke smiled just thinking about her pitch yesterday. "Well, it turns out they invited thirty-six of us to come present."

"So few?" Delbrina asked.

At the same time, Noemi said, "So many?"

"Few enough to be honored that they invited me to present," Brooke said. "But enough to know better than to get my hopes up. Regardless of what happens, I'm glad I went. It was quite the experience presenting to executives at a department store as big as Van Zandt."

"*The* biggest in the nation," Noemi interrupted.

"Okay, *the biggest*. They had twelve of us present a day, and we each got twenty minutes to show our portfolio and talk about what kind of things we'd include in a clothing line if they chose to feature us in next year's spring catalog, just like we had planned. But then they took an extra ten minutes asking questions about our business size and production levels, online and brick and mortar stores, and manufacturing."

"How did it go?" Noemi asked.

"I was on top of my game," Brooke said, smiling. She had done even better than she had all the times she'd run through it in her head during the days leading up to it.

"And," Delbrina said, drawing out the word, "what we really want to know is how was the competition? Were they cutthroat?"

Brooke laughed. "They had a reception for us, and there were only a few I hadn't met before. Not a single label sent a marketing rep— there were only designers who were also the owners of their labels. These people are my friends, my mentors, and my peers. They're all amazing, and I'm sure they all did well."

Getting her designs into a department store chain like Van Zandt had always been Brooke's dream, and with this invitation to demo, Van Zandt was also offering to feature the label. Everything she had been doing with her business — from her online store to her product in boutiques to the industry relationships she nurtured, and even to her store here in Nestled Hollow— had been, at least in part, to attract the attention of a business like Van Zandt.

But that was true for all thirty-six people who had

presented to them, so spending time daydreaming about it wasn't wise. Spending time working toward building her business was.

"I'm sure I won't hear back for a few weeks, though, so let's get down to business." She glanced down at her buzzing phone, her brow crinkled. She had spent all day yesterday in the green room at Van Zandt with Ian, as they had each waited for their turn to present. They didn't talk nearly often enough to warrant a phone call again so soon. She slid to answer the call, pressed the speaker phone, and said, "Hello, Ian! Miss me already?"

"Have you thought any more about the partnership I proposed? Our businesses would combine beautifully. We'd work together pretty well, too."

"You know I love you, Ian. But my answer is still no—I'm a lone wolf; always will be."

"I appreciate your 'no.' I respect your 'no' just like I respect you. But I think it's the wrong answer."

Brooke smiled at his persistence. On anyone else, it might be annoying. But Ian was just so darn likable that it was hard to get annoyed at anything he did. "I know you do. Thank you again for the offer."

"Don't worry, I'll convince you yet."

"I don't doubt that you'll try."

As soon as Brooke hung up the phone, Noemi said, "You never told us that you got a business offer. Do you want to discuss it?"

"I didn't tell you because it was irrelevant. I'm not interested in a partnership."

"Why?" Noemi asked. "Because you're worried the two of you might get romantically involved?"

"Me and Ian?" Brooke laughed. "No. He's...he's not my type and very much taken."

"Then why?" Delbrina asked. "You'd grow your business and extend your reach. Ian seems like a nice guy. And he designs suits, which is an area where we're weak. With a partnership, many of the costs and efforts would be split in half. And you could utilize each other's manufacturers when one has downtime."

Brooke shook her head. "My dad always taught me to never merge with a company that's the same size as yours. And he's one of the best there is at growing businesses."

Delbrina and Noemi nodded. They both knew who her dad was— most people did, even if they didn't know she was his daughter— and with his success, people rightly assumed that her dad knew his stuff. He'd always taught her that it never worked out if you joined as equals. Someone had to take the lead, to make the hard decisions when two partners wouldn't agree. And unless you were the bigger business, the name of your own business— the one you created from the ground up— was likely to disappear.

Her phone buzzed again and she shook her head when she saw who it was. She touched *Accept* and put the phone to her ear. "When you said you'd keep trying to convince me, I didn't think you meant every five minutes."

"They've chosen." Ian's voice came out with barely restrained excitement.

"Who has?"

"Van Zandt!"

Brooke stood up from her stool. "So soon? I thought it would be weeks!"

"They said there were five standouts. It made their choice easy. Are you checking your email? Check your email already!"

Brooke raced to the standing table with the computer, turned the phone on speaker, and set it beside the computer. She put the password into the login screen, then logged into her email. The email from Van Zandt Corporate was right at the top, the words *Five Finalists Chosen* in the subject line jumping out at her.

Her hand hovered over the mouse, suddenly unsure if she wanted to click. She had thought she'd been okay with whatever answer she got from them, but now that the list was here, she wasn't sure she was ready to hear if she didn't make the cut.

"Click it!" Delbrina and Noemi shouted at the same time.

So she clicked the button and scanned through the email, none of the words sinking in until she saw *Brooke McClellan with By the Brooke* in the list of five. She gasped and tried to focus on the lines above it, just to confirm that this was, indeed, the list of finalists and not the list of people they were taking out of the running. She could barely focus, though. The screaming and jumping of Delbrina and Noemi confirmed that she was a finalist. And right below her name was *Ian Bancroft with Bancroft Limited.*

"I made the top five!" she shouted. "Ian, we both made the top five!" She spun around and wrapped her arms around Noemi and Delbrina, and they all jumped up and down in a difficult-to-maintain hug, screaming, Ian squealing his excitement through the phone.

Breathless, Brooke collapsed into the nearest chair. "I can't believe they chose my brand. This is so huge. I've spent countless hours of my life dreaming of this, but I still can't wrap my head around it."

"I'll contact our manufacturer," Noemi said, "and have Dave give us some numbers on what kind of output he could get in the space we have if we let him hire as many employees as he wants. And I'll check with outsourcing some sewing, too, if ours isn't enough."

Brooke nodded.

"And I'll let our designer know that this next lookbook needs to knock it out of the park," Delbrina added.

Item after item kept flying onto Brooke's mental to-do list as the adrenaline from the news flowed through her.

She stood up and went to the computer to read the rest of the email.

"I know you didn't go and forget that I am on the phone," Ian said.

"Ian," Brooke said, "after news like this, I didn't even remember where I was."

He laughed. "That's why it took me a good five minutes after I saw the email before I called you. Did you see the attached file? That's a list of the things they want us to prepare before the next meeting when they'll cut the list down further. It's, uh...it's long. And they're giving us three weeks."

"Three weeks?!"

"It's insane," Ian said. "And I have my fashion show right in the middle of that three weeks. You'll still come help, right?"

"You know me well enough to know I wouldn't bail on you."

"You're the best kind of people there is. Check out their list. You make sure to let me know if you want to work together on any of it."

With that tone of voice, his implication came through loud and clear. "Ha, ha, Ian. My answer is still no."

"It was worth a try. You know where to find me if it changes to a yes."

After she hung up, Noemi and Delbrina squealed. "You did it!" Noemi shouted. "You made the top five!"

Brooke buzzed with energy and practically floated with excitement. "I've been dreaming about this since I was four and made my Barbie a dress out of paper towels and Scotch tape."

The bell on the front door *dinged* and Brooke stepped to where she could see through the doorway to the shop. "Whitney! It's so good to see you!" Brooke said as she rushed forward to greet her friend. "Come on back here." Brooke led her to the padded chairs that were set in a little conversation cluster on the rug in one of the corners and they both sat down as Brooke tried to calm her breathing. "How was Sacramento?"

"It was great!" Whitney said. "I love watching Eli run team-building groups."

"And I bet you're enjoying all the extra time with him, too."

Whitney blushed. "Yeah, that too. How was New York?"

"It was good. I went to a fun party, made some connections, and even met a couple of people who are corporate sales reps."

"That's fantastic! Do you think anything will come of it?"

Brooke shrugged. "Hard to say. I mean I hope so, but this is a pretty competitive business."

"So," Whitney said, drawing the word out, "did you go on any fun dates while you were there?"

"Oh yeah," Noemi said, "I can't believe we forgot to ask if you went on a date with Travis."

Delbrina shook her head. "Travis is the guy in Austin. Saloy is the one in New York."

Brooke chuckled. "Saloy is in Los Angeles." She turned back to Whitney. "Sadly, no. I often go on a date with *Rennen* when I'm in New York, but he met someone new and decided he wanted to be exclusive with them."

"So what I'm hearing is that you could really use a date."

Brooke could see the mischievousness in her friend's expression. "Whitney, no."

Whitney held up her hands. "Don't worry, I didn't set you up on a blind date or anything like that. I know how annoying that can be. I was just thinking it might be fun to have you and a date double with me and Eli for an early dinner tonight. You know, someone from town maybe."

"I am more than happy to join the two of you for dinner tonight. *Without a date.* I've been the third wheel with you and Eli plenty of times before and I don't mind it at all."

"I'm not saying you should marry someone from town or anything. I'm just saying it might be fun to go out as couples."

"I don't date people from town. I've seen how it is. If you go out on one date, people in town already start rooting for you before you've even decided if you want a second date. And then if you did decide to keep dating them, once you eventually stop dating, you'd still see them all the time and then things get awkward."

"It's supposed to be 'if' you stop dating," Whitney said. "Not 'when.'"

"Oh, honey," Delbrina said, "you might as well give up. Brooke doesn't date anyone exclusively, let alone long-term."

Whitney raised a questioning eyebrow. She hadn't ever pressed Brooke for more information, even though Brooke had pushed Whitney quite a bit when she first started dating Eli. She probably owed her an explanation. She blew out a deep breath. "Being married holds you back. People have different opinions on everything— it's normal and natural. So anytime you have to make a decision, it slows things down and complicates everything. It limits you. It pins you down. There's not as much freedom to make the tough choices. It's true in business and it's true in life."

"My man can pin me down anytime he likes," Delbrina said, and high-fived Noemi.

"Have you *never* been in an exclusive relationship?" Whitney asked disbelief all across her face.

Brooke shook her head. "Nope. I need to be free to make all decisions. It's one of the few things my parents ever agreed on and something that both their short-lived marriage and their long, successful careers have backed up."

To Whitney's credit, she didn't try to convince Brooke otherwise. That's one of the things Brooke loved best about her friend— she didn't just assume that since she'd found love that she should make it her mission to convince everyone else that they should, too. Whitney had spent enough time spurning dates herself that she seemed to understand that pushing someone wouldn't work. "I get it. So are we on for the three of us tonight at Back Porch Grill?"

"I wouldn't miss it for the world."

three

COLE

Cole put the last of the pork chops in a pan to brown, the tomato-lemonade sauce they would bake in already prepared in a bowl beside him, the sound of his sous chef Hani chopping vegetables behind him. In a town with only three restaurants, he got plenty of chances to make a variety of menu items. He had staples on his menu that would always be there, of course, but he made sure that there was one new item every night. It kept people from getting tired of eating the same things, and he got to stretch his skills and creativity daily.

"This is a pretty big batch of tortellini soup you've got me making, Chef," Hani said. "Are you taking some to the shelter in Mountain Springs or to people in town?"

"People in town. There are several who are recovering

from sicknesses or surgeries. They could all use a helping hand."

"So, Boss," Hani said, and Cole turned to glance at the twenty-two-year-old when he heard the tentative excitement in the kid's voice. "Any chance you can let me off on Saturday night? I know I'm scheduled, but some tickets to Scattered Serenity just fell into my lap and it's Tehya's favorite band. I think she might be the one, Boss."

"You thought Bree was the one." Cole cut three red peppers in half and then started slicing the chilies for the Romesco sauce.

"Nah. I was wrong about that. But Tehya. Man, I think she could be the one for real."

Cole grunted. He had no problem at all with employees requesting time off—when they did it before he made the schedule. He wiped off his hands then grabbed his phone and brought up the calendar, scrutinizing everything he had listed for both the restaurant and his daughter before setting it back on its shelf. "I'll tell you what. Work the lunch shift on Saturday, and you can take the night off."

Hani's grin was so wide it was probably blinding people three blocks away. Cole cut the ends off a few cloves of garlic and after a pause, Hani said, "Do you think you'll ever find 'the one,' Boss?"

Cole eyed Hani. This was not a subject he liked to discuss. He pulled out a sheet pan and placed the red peppers, chilies, and garlic on it, and drizzled olive oil on them. "I already did."

"Right," Hani said. "But I meant after Amanda."

Cole had loved Amanda more than anything. Her dying wish had been for him to find someone else, but that had become rather complicated. "I don't know, Hani. Guess you'll have to stick around to find out."

Cole put the pan in the broiler and then looked out the pass-through when the bell on the front door dinged. He smiled when he saw Samantha. Then he wiped his hands on a towel, grabbed her after-school snack, and headed to the bar straight out from the pass-through where his daughter always sat to do homework.

"Daddy!" she said as she dropped her backpack on a bar stool and ran to hug him.

"How's my Samster? And how was good ole Nestled Hollow Elementary on this fine day?"

"Good and good," Samantha said as she climbed onto the stool. Cole put the bowl of fruit down in front of her and sat on the stool next to her. She grabbed the fork and stabbed a piece of honeydew. "Remember how Mrs. Alvarez said that she wanted us to be the best fourth graders at cursive that Nestled Hollow has ever seen?"

Cole nodded.

"Well, today, she said that we were! And she stuck my cursive assignment to the whiteboard as the 'shining example.'"

"That's my girl," he said and met her high-five.

She stuck the chunk of melon in her mouth and mumbled around it, "How's work?"

"Five people ordered the *Sam's Special* at lunch today. Who knew that grilled peanut butter, jelly, and banana would be such a hit?"

Sam swallowed and held up a finger. "'Banana Peanut Butter Jelly Rub Your Belly.' And *I* did. Oh, and I already have an idea for tomorrow's *Sam's Special*. 'Lip Smack 'n' Cheese.' It's your regular mac and cheese, but with bacon." She made a show of licking her lips and rubbing her stomach. "And you should use that pasta that looks like smiley faces." She stuck a grape in her mouth. "And then bring some home for dinner."

"How did I get so lucky to have such a brilliantly creative daughter?"

She shrugged. "Because God loves you." Then she took a bite of cantaloupe.

"Your birthday is coming up in just over a month. Have you thought about what you want to do at your party? It's a pretty big deal to turn ten."

Cole was surprised at how quickly the smile dropped from Sam's face and her shoulders fell. She pushed the fruit around in her bowl with her fork. "I was thinking about not having a party this year."

"Why?" Cole asked. "You love birthday parties." He

paused a moment, then asked, "Has someone in school been mean?"

Sam shook her head.

"Then what?"

She lifted one shoulder in a shrug. "Maybe I'm too old for parties."

"Boss," Hani called out from the kitchen, "you've got smoke coming out of your oven."

He closed his eyes. He'd completely forgotten that he'd put that tray into broil. "Just take the pan out of the oven," he called out. "You're not too old for parties. What's the real reason?"

Sam just shook her head and looked down, clearly not wanting to tell him why. He couldn't even begin to guess and had no idea what questions to ask to get her to open up.

"Boss?" Hani said, sounding worried. "They're a little black."

Cole squinted at Samantha, trying desperately to see through what she was showing on the surface to what lay behind it, but came up with nothing. "I've got to go toss those before they stink up the place, but let's talk more about this later, okay?"

Sam nodded.

Cole took the tray outside and dumped its contents into the dumpster. As he cut new peppers and chilies and garlic, he watched Sam through the pass-through. She had pushed her snack aside and gotten out her book, a homework sheet, and a pencil, but she wasn't getting much done. She was mostly doodling in the margins of her homework, resting her head on her hand, and generally looking less than enthused.

Cole wished he knew how to help her. It was rough being her only parent— there was so much he didn't understand and so many areas where he felt inadequate. He had never thought he'd be a single dad trying to raise a daughter on his own, but here he was.

After he added a couple of slices of olive oil-brushed artisan bread on the pan under the broiler and moved the last of the pork chops from the frying pan to the baking pan, he studied Sam and tried to think of ways he could start a conversation with her about her birthday.

The bell on the door sounded and Brooke walked in. A feeling of peace washed over him, and he knew things would be okay even before he saw the smile spread across Sam's face at seeing Brooke.

Brooke had first walked into Back Porch Grill just a couple of months after Amanda died, and she'd been a godsend ever since. She'd been a good friend to both him and Sam when they had needed it most. Even though he worried about Sam getting too attached to Brooke, it was times like these that he was so grateful for Brooke's help.

He whistled as he poured the sauce over the pork chops, covered the pan with foil, and placed it in the oven to cook for the next ninety minutes. He glanced out at the two of them as he put all the ingredients in the food processor to finish the Romesco sauce while he was pan-frying chicken for paella, and each time, the two were laughing and connecting.

Brooke must've asked about the book that Samantha was reading, because she picked it up and showed it to Brooke and started pointing out things on the cover, then flipped to the page she was on. Brooke seemed to always have insider knowledge about how people were feeling, so he knew it wouldn't take long for her to realize that something was bothering Sam and to find a way to get her to talk about it.

Not ten minutes later, Cole looked through the opening and saw the magic happen. "Bingo."

"What's that, Chef?" Hani asked.

He stirred the paella as the wine finished cooking down and added the remaining ingredients, nestled the chicken into the rice, then covered the dish. "Something's bothering Sam. Brooke, of course, realized that, and she and Sam just moved to a booth to chat more. She'll have it figured out in no time."

"That's great, Boss!"

Hani looked like he had more to say but had already turned back to the chicken he was prepping, so Cole said, "Spit it out, Hani."

"Nothin', Boss. Brooke's just a good person to have

around, that's all I'm sayin'."

Cole nodded. "That she is."

Over the next forty-five minutes, as Cole and Hani rushed to get the last of the prep done before the dinner crowd started showing up, he didn't get nearly as many chances to watch Sam and Brooke through the opening.

But every time he glanced out, he noticed Sam was doing better and better, until the two of them were laughing again and Sam looked like she was making progress on her homework. His daughter loved the days when Brooke came in because then she didn't have to come back to the chaos of the kitchens to work on her homework.

Cole said hello to his hostess, Morgan, and his waiter and waitress for the night, Dex and Jamie, and Heather, the cook who would be Hani's assistant for the night, when they came into the kitchens to clock in. He told them about the specials and let them each try the finished paella so they could describe it to the customers. Then he kept an eye on the front door for his mother-in-law as he finished up the food prep and the first few dinner customers trickled in.

A handful of tables had guests seated when Susan, Amanda's mom, walked through the front door. Cole wiped his hands on a towel, took off his apron, asked Hani to cover everything for a few minutes, and headed out to the lobby to greet her.

There were lots of painful memories he'd had to work his way through to stay in Nestled Hollow, but having Samantha's grandma close had been one of the many benefits of sticking with it. She wasn't exactly the warmest, most comforting grandma, nor was she big on conversation, but she loved Sam and gave her a home environment to hang out in until Cole got off work. As their only relative within driving distance of Nestled Hollow, Sam adored her.

When he walked into the dining area, he could see that Sam and Brooke were finishing up their conversation and Sam had just begun loading up her backpack with all her things.

"Thank you for coming to get Sam," he told Susan.

She nodded, but she seemed hesitant, and Cole knew that meant she had something to say that she wasn't saying.

"What is it, Susan? Would you prefer she not go to your house tonight?"

"You know I don't mind having her over," Susan said. Then she let out a huge breath. "Actually, there is something I've been meaning to talk with you about. Amanda didn't want you to still be a single dad, raising Samantha on your own."

"I know," Cole said, not meeting her eyes.

"She wanted you to have a wife again. She wanted Sam to have a mother."

Three years ago, as he'd lain on the bed next to Amanda, holding her hand in the last few hours before cancer took her, he'd been opening his mouth to promise her that he'd never so much as date another person— that he'd stay true to her until the very end.

But before he'd gotten a chance, she'd spoken in a voice more fierce and strong and sure than he'd heard from her in weeks. "You promise me you'll get remarried," she'd said. Cole had been so surprised by it that he hadn't gotten a chance to respond before she went on. "I love you too much to see you spending the rest of your life alone. And not only that, our daughter deserves to have a mother. Give her one."

"I don't know if I can," he'd managed to croak out. And truly, he hadn't. Back then, he hadn't fathomed he'd ever be able to imagine himself with anyone else.

After using so much energy to get out her request, Amanda's voice had gone back to its weakened, quiet rasp. "Of course, you don't think you can right now. But your grief won't always be so strong. One day, it'll seem possible. Three years," she'd said, looking into his eyes like she could burn her wishes into his will. "Three years and I want you to be married. Promise me?"

He'd searched her eyes, wondering how he could make a promise like that.

"It's important, Cole. Please promise me."

After squeezing her hand, he'd made the promise.

He thought of the promise often, especially at times like today, when Sam needed someone who could figure out what was really bothering her. It hurt to know he hadn't kept that promise. Especially since the three-year mark passed a month ago. Just like Amanda had guessed, he had reached the point where he knew he could marry someone else. She probably hadn't guessed how much more complicated things would get the second time around.

Actually, finding someone else wasn't the issue. There were so many more factors in play than that.

"I know it's tough," Susan said. "There's a reason why I never remarried after my Harold died. But tough or not, you need to put dating on your schedule."

"I know," Cole said, feeling the familiar weight of his promise settling on him.

"I love being her grandma," Susan said, "but I can't be her mom."

They both glanced over as Brooke and Sam hugged each other before Sam hefted on her backpack.

"Grandma!" Sam said as she ran to her and wrapped her arms around Susan's waist in a quick hug.

Cole crouched down to Sam's height. "You doing good, sweetie?"

"Ten out of ten," she said, holding both thumbs up.

He smiled, hugged her, and said, "I'll be by to pick you up at seven. And I'll bring something tasty for dinner."

As the two of them left, Cole glanced around for Brooke. She had slipped into a booth across from Whitney and Eli, and she waved him over and patted the seat next to her.

He walked over and slid into the seat. "Hello, Whitney, Eli. It's good to see you." He turned to Brooke. "I see you got missing my food."

"It's the real reason I had to get an earlier flight back."

"Yeah, I've heard that New York is lacking in good restaurants."

"They may have some flash, but they've got nothing on Back Porch Grill."

Cole knew she was just saying that because she was Brooke. But it still made him feel good.

"I know it's a good ninety percent of the reason why I moved here," Eli said, and Whitney smacked his shoulder with the back of her hand. Eli laughed. "Okay, okay, it was only like four percent of the reason, but it's a very tasty four percent."

"Thanks for hanging out with Sam. Did you happen to find out what was bothering her?"

Brooke nodded. "Do you remember a picture book called *Princess Samantha's Perfect Party*?"

Cole racked his brain. "I think so."

"It's a book her mom used to read to her at night. It was about a girl— Princess Samantha— who made a wish to have the perfect party. It sounds like it was a pretty elaborate party. Anyway, in the book, it was Princess Samantha's tenth birthday, and since the princess and Sam had the same name, her mom always promised that you'd have a party like that for her when she turned ten. So, as you can imagine, thoughts of turning ten kind of make her miss her mom."

Huh. He was going to have to see if he could find that book. "How'd you get her smiling and laughing again after?"

Brooke lifted a shoulder in a shrug. "I just listened as she told me how much she loved her mom, then listened some more as she told me about all the fun things they did together, then that morphed into funny things until we were both laughing pretty hard."

"You, Brooke, are a gift."

She grinned. "What are best friends for?"

"Hey," Whitney said. "I thought *I* was your best friend."

"You're my best womanly friend." She placed a hand on his arm. "Cole's my best manly friend."

Cole had to tamp down both the feeling her touch sent zinging through him and the thrill her words gave him like he always did. And as grateful as he was for her right now, he needed to get some distance if he wanted to keep his resistance at full power.

He glanced at his watch and then put both hands on the table and pushed himself to stand. "I've got to make sure everything's set in the kitchen then go deliver some meals so I can get home to Sam. You three have a wonderful dinner."

Brooke gave him a smile that would warm even the coldest nights. He let himself genuinely return her smile to show his immense gratitude before pushing the feelings he had for her away again. It didn't matter how attracted he was to Brooke; they could never be more than friends.

BROOKE

Brooke breathed in the aroma of freshly ground coffee as she stepped into Love a Latte. The smell itself woke up her senses and made her feel like maybe she could accomplish today.

"Well, look at you," the woman said as Brooke stepped up to the counter. "You're practically glowing, especially for six a.m. I take it you've had a good morning?"

"Hey, Tory. I'm glowing?" Apparently, yesterday's news of making the top five was still fresh enough. "Are you sure you aren't misinterpreting it as me collapsing under the weight of my to-do list?"

Tory laughed, then scrutinized Brooke like she always did as she decided what kind of drink Brooke needed. "Triple shot latte?"

"Or four."

"I'll tell you what. When I leave at eight-thirty to take my kiddos to school, I'll stop by Best Dressed with a fresh cup."

"Whatever they're paying you, Tory, it isn't enough." It had been their running joke since the first time Brooke had walked into the shop before she'd known that Tory was the owner and that there was no mystical "they" writing her a paycheck. She paid for her drinks and slipped a twenty dollar bill in the tip jar when Tory wasn't looking.

As Brooke walked down the still-dark Main Street toward Best Dressed, everything ran through her head that she needed to do to prepare for her next presentation at Van Zandt's along with everything that needed to happen for normal day-to-day operations of her business. She'd had a meeting with her team yesterday, and they'd hammered a lot of it out and divided many of the tasks.

But when she'd gone back to work after her dinner with Whitney and Eli last night to work, and while she'd been home sleeping, her brain kept adding more and more things to the list. Now the "list" in her brain was a jumbled mess that she needed to get down on paper and hopefully Delbrina and Noemi could work their magic and form it into a plan.

Even without seeing their plan, she knew it would be pretty impossible to meet, even with her incredible team.

By the time Delbrina and Noemi came in at nine, she

had a master list of all the things that had come to her mind, scribbled down and covering the page. They talked about all the normal business items first, and then the two of them took her messy notes and combined them with the list of things Van Zandt had requested.

Brooke looked over the list. "We also need to deal with the fact that I already have a trip to L.A. planned right in the middle of all this."

"Why are they only giving us three weeks to prepare?" Noemi asked. "They hadn't even planned to come up with the five finalists so quickly. Surely they had more days worked into their timetable."

"I suspect the three weeks is less about their timetable and more about seeing what we can accomplish in such a short period. The tight deadline itself might make their decision easier. We'll just have to work hard and make it happen."

"My biggest worry is this," Delbrina said, reaching across the table and tapping the fourth item in Van Zandt's list. "*Designing something that stays true to your brand, but at the same time is very different from anything you've done.* That's going to be difficult. Your brand is already quite diverse, and coming up with something so different on such a quick timetable is going to be tougher than a two-dollar steak."

"Do you have any ideas yet?" Noemi asked.

Brooke shook her head. "Nothing. It's my biggest

worry, too. I might just spend the day sketching designs, or even surfing the web for interesting people, and hope that inspiration hits."

The bell on the front door rang, even though it wasn't time for the shop to open yet, and she leaned out from the design table they always met around to see who it was.

"Cole! Come on back!"

Her friend looked happy. Excited. Slightly impressed with himself. And hopeful. Tory would probably even say he was "glowing" too.

Brooke loved that her and her team's offices, their design and production areas, meeting areas, and even some storage space were all open, one area flowing into another with no walls dividing things up. But as usual, when Cole stepped into the area, he looked overwhelmed at everything that was going on in the big space.

He glanced at all the papers they had spread on the design table. "Am I coming at a bad time? I can come back."

"Since I've never seen you outside of the walls of the restaurant at this time of day, I'd say you must be pretty excited about what you've got in your hands. Sit down and spill."

Cole pulled one of the empty stools closer to Brooke's and set a book down on the table, grinning. "I found it."

Brooke ran her fingers across the title, *Princess Samantha's Perfect Party*. She smiled at him. "Nice work."

"I can see why this was important to her. Everything in this story is stuff Sam would go crazy for." He looked down at the book for a moment, running his big strong finger across the delicate images on the cover. "Why wouldn't Sam just ask me to give her this party?"

"Because she knows that all of this isn't really up your alley."

He looked down at the table. "She's my daughter. If anything, all the tea parties I've attended and all the times I've played Barbies should've let her know that I'd do anything for her. I even let her paint my toenails and put bows in my hair."

Brooke looked up and down at her broad-shouldered friend with his big hands and facial scruff and laughed at the mental image of bows in his hair and sparkly polish on his toes. "She knows that you'd do anything for her. I think that she just didn't want to ask you to do something so far out of your comfort zone."

"I want to surprise her with this party. Do you think I can pull it off?"

Brooke opened the book and started reading through the story. It was a story about a princess who just really wanted to feel loved. So when her fairy godmother showed up to ask her what she most wanted, she said that she wanted a party that all of her friends would enjoy. It told about how the two of them planned for the princess to invite ten dukes and ten duchesses, and how they would all arrive for the party in a shiny stagecoach, and they would all be lifted to the top of a tower and slide down a giant slide into the courtyard where the party would take place.

The invitations were fancy, the food was fancy, the decorations were fancy, and the princess wore a fluffy, shimmering dress with sparkly ribbons in her hair, and had on glittery shoes. And the activities were going to be the most fun that any of the dukes and duchesses had ever experienced.

She met her friend's eyes and could see that he wanted to make this party every bit as magical as the book made it seem. She also saw the sadness in his eyes that his daughter didn't have her mother for this, and he wanted to give her something just as grand as if her mom were still alive. He was great at scheduling everything into his life that needed to fit, and he was very capable when it came to projects. But there was no way he was going to come up with the initial plan on his own.

She also knew that together, they *could* come up with that plan. *If* she could find a way to fit it in with all she had to do.

There were many things that her parents had taught her about running a business. But there was one thing that they taught her that they hadn't meant to teach her— that people matter more than businesses.

Over and over as she grew up, she saw both of her parents sacrificing relationships with people when those relationships took them away from their business goals. Deep down, she knew that no success in business would make up for failed relationships. As a teen, she had vowed to put people first.

Especially people like Samantha. Brooke had connected with her the first time she'd met her, back when Sam had just started first grade and she saw her struggling with reading as she sat in a booth one afternoon at Back Porch Grill. And people like Cole, who she'd developed a fast friendship with.

She took a glance at all the to-do lists spread across the table and took a slow, deep breath to calm the stress bubbling up inside her. Then she turned to Cole. "With my help, I think we can come up with a plan."

"Really?" There was a moment of hesitation on his face that Brooke was sure she'd caught before excitement shone in his eyes again, followed quickly by uncertainty as he glanced at her papers. "You're not too busy?"

"Not for this. But Cole?"

He met her eyes.

"Don't make it a surprise party."

Shock crossed his face. "Why?"

"Honey," Delbrina said, "this party is for your daughter, not for you, right?"

He nodded.

"Surprises are a gift for the person doing the surprising, not the person being surprised."

Cole looked confused. And like her employees always did, even on non-business matters, they jumped in to give their opinions.

"Think about it," Noemi said. "The bulk of the excitement comes in all the planning and the anticipation. Trust me: she'll have ten times the fun planning this party with you than she will if you are away from her more than usual, keeping secrets until a party is sprung on her that she hadn't had time to get properly excited about."

Cole looked to Brooke for confirmation. "They're right. You can feel it."

He nodded. "Thank you. All of you. She's going to love this." He pulled out his phone and brought up his calendar. "Sam has piano lessons until six today. Do you think we could meet with her tonight around seven to make plans?"

Brooke said, "I'd love to," and figured she'd just have to find a way to make it work later.

As they stood up and she walked him through the storefront to the front door, he said, "I never asked—how was your trip to New York?"

She smiled. "It was a lot of fun. I met some cool people, went to a fun party, and got some great advice during lunch with a fellow designer."

After saying goodbye, she stopped in her tracks when she came back into the offices and saw the looks on Noemi's and Delbrina's faces. "What?"

"Why don't you let anyone here know how successful you are?" Noemi asked, a hand on her hip.

Delbrina put her hand on her hip, too, the two of them looking remarkably similar for how different each woman was. "You just made the top five designers being considered by Van Zandt! And you didn't say boo to Whitney yesterday or Cole today. You told both you just went to a party and met some people."

"Which is completely true."

"You could be a celebrity here," Noemi said. "I'd sell my soul to be as successful and well-known as you."

"And," Delbrina added, "if you let them know what was going on, they would understand when you've got too much on your plate to add something else."

"People are important," Brooke said as she went back to the design table. "This party is important. And I like small-town life. I grew up in New York and Los Angeles and Paris. I've lived the big city life, and I still get to be Big City Brooke every couple of weeks. It's nice. I enjoy it, obviously.

"But this place"— She spread her arms wide, encompassing the whole town before picking up her pen. "This place fits. I like who I am here. My parents gave me the education and the experiences to support what I'm good at and passionate about. But here is where I'm home. Nestled Hollow is where I'm *me*. I don't want any successes outside of Nestled Hollow to change things here."

Both of her employees nodded like they understood, even if they didn't agree.

"Now let's get to work— we've got a lot of things to get done in a small amount of time."

five

COLE

Cole walked with Samantha up Brooke's sidewalk toward her front door, Sam holding his hand and clutching the book, a skip in her step. The sun was just setting, and the golden skies cast a shade of gold on everything. It was barely spring, yet Brooke already had flowers popping up in her flower beds. As usual, her entire yard looked immaculate, even with the grass still more brown from winter than green from the beginning of spring.

They knocked on the door and waited. When Brooke didn't come to the door, he knocked again, more loudly this time. Still, she didn't come to the door. He was just reaching for his phone to call her when she pulled into the driveway. The garage door opened and she parked inside, the door shutting behind her. Then, moments later, she opened the front door, her face flushed from rushing.

"I'm so sorry I'm late. There were things at work that had to be done before I left, and I just couldn't quite finish in time. Come in, come in."

"Is tonight a bad night for this?" Cole asked. "If you're too busy"—

"I'm not too busy for this," she said as she led them through the living room and into the dining room that was open to the kitchen.

Sam had been giddy when he'd told her about the plan to work with Brooke to recreate Princess Samantha's Perfect Party. Finding out that they'd be planning the party at Brooke's house had been the frosting on the cake.

Cole figured that everyone's house probably reflected who they were, but Brooke's house always felt like it was more *her* than any other house reflected its owner. All the furnishings, the art, the way everything was arranged— all were fashionable and polished, just like she was. But unlike other nice homes that he'd been in, Brooke's felt comfortable and inviting. Like guests were welcome anywhere in her house and could stay as long as they'd like. He always felt at peace in her home.

He never did get how she managed to afford it all, though. Especially because she had a couple of employees working for her whose salaries she had to pay, too. Plus, she took vacations all across the country just to go to parties, and that had to get expensive.

Sure, tourists and people from neighboring towns came to Nestled Hollow all the time, but even with them, there were only so many fancy dresses people needed. He'd heard her talk about selling her dresses in boutique shops in other places. He had no idea what a boutique shop was, but maybe that's what kept her afloat.

As they took seats around Brooke's table, Sam reverently placed the book on the table.

"How'd your book report go?" Brooke asked.

Sam smiled. "Remember how one of your suggestions was to tell about the adventure the kids went on in the book like I was a news reporter on TV, reporting about the story? Well, I decided to do that and practiced in front of my dad like a gazillion times last night, so when I got up in front of my class, I wasn't even nervous."

Cole beamed at Sam. "She even threw in an interview with the main character, who she also played, which was humorous and, if I might say, pretty brilliant."

"My class even laughed at all the right places."

Brooke gave Sam a high five, and said, "Hard work and preparation pay off every time. I'm proud of you for putting so much into it."

Brooke had first stepped into their lives a few months after Amanda died. Both he and Sam had been drowning and neither of them knew how to help the other. Brooke came along and reached a hand out to both of them, pulling them right out of the water.

It had made a huge difference to Samantha to have a woman who she could talk with and have as an example. Sam idolized Brooke. As much as he loved the two of them doing things together, it was hard on Samantha every time Brooke was gone. And she left a lot. Sam already didn't have a mom and needed some stability in her life. The older Samantha got, the worse it seemed to get.

"Okay, let me tell you about this book," Sam said as she opened to the first page and ran her hands from the middle out to the sides, both spreading the pages out flatter and showing them off like a prize. "So this girl is Princess Samantha, and she's pretty sad. I know you wouldn't think it'd be this way, but she's actually pretty lonely as the princess, and so she makes a wish on that star that she'll feel loved."

She flipped to the next page. "And then *boom!* This fairy godmother appears, and she's super nice, and they decide that for Princess Samantha's tenth birthday, which was coming up soon, they would have a massive awesome party and invite lots of kids. And they would make the party so much fun that all the kids would have a blast, and then she wouldn't be lonely and she'd feel loved."

As Sam went through the story, she flipped to each page, sometimes telling just a bit, sometimes pausing to point out the expression on Princess Samantha's face, and sometimes telling even more than the words on the page told.

"So first, they decided that since she was turning ten, they should invite ten dukes and ten duchesses to the party. And guess what? You're not even going to believe this. Not counting me, there are ten girls and ten boys in my class!" She made a motion of her head exploding. "That was the first thing I noticed when we all found our seats on the first day of fourth grade."

Sam hadn't even mentioned that to Cole. It pained him to know that his little girl had been thinking specifically about this party for what, a little over six months? And each time she'd thought about it, she had thought it would never happen, and each time it would make her miss her mom even more. All this time and he hadn't even known.

Brooke laughed. "Well, I guess you've got the guest list down already then." She wrote *Guest list* on her paper, then put a big check mark next to it.

The look of bliss on Sam's face right now, though, was one that Cole wished he could bottle and keep for emergencies.

Sam flipped to the next page. "So then they made these invitations that were beautiful and sparkly. But I don't think we should make ours sparkly, because it turns out that a lot of boys don't like it when they get glitter stuck to them. Weird, I know. Whenever I see a random piece of glitter sparkling on my arm or face, I just know the day is going to be magical." She shrugged her shoulders. "But my dad always says that you don't have to understand why people feel a certain way to show respect for those feelings. So no glitter it is!"

Cole chuckled. Sam always sounded so grown up whenever she repeated things he'd said. And the moments when she learned the things he always hoped she'd learn from him were so much better than the times she learned things from him he wished she hadn't. He felt Brooke's eyes on him and glanced over to see an expression he couldn't quite interpret. Neither of them looked away, so he kept trying to guess.

And then Sam flipped to the next page, where she told about how a unicorn-drawn carriage brought all of the kids to the party, and whatever spell had kept them looking at each other was broken.

She flipped the page again, and the picture showed a magical platform that raised the kids to a high tower, where they slid down a slide to get to the courtyard where the party would happen.

"I've got it," Cole said. "I take warm soup to Nate's construction crew on cold days often, and he said if I ever needed a favor to just ask. I bet he'd be willing to make a kind of platform. Then we could put you on it, and have it raise you up like an angel floating up into the sky, and then everyone can sing happy birthday to you."

Samantha raised a hand like a stop sign and said, "Dad, no," in her firmest voice. "This book is not about Princess Samantha getting everybody to do cool things for her. It's about a girl who plans a party for *everyone* to have fun and feel special and loved. The whole point of the story is to make sure all the dukes and duchesses have a great time. That's what makes the princess have the perfect day."

He leaned over and kissed the top of her head. "You're a cool girl, Samster."

As Sam told more of the story, Brooke wrote each of the items on her list.

"And this is the sad part of the story," Sam said. "On the day of the party, the fairy godmother got sick! But there was so much that needed to be done for the party that day, so they could no longer do all the things they had planned.

"But don't get too worried like I always did—the story ended up being okay because all the dukes and duchesses that the princess had invited helped to pull it off, which was fun for everyone, and that's actually what made the princess feel loved."

Sam ran her fingers across the fairy godmother who was lying in a bed, looking miserable, a thermometer in her mouth. "When my mom used to read me this story, she told me we would have a party like this when I turned ten, but I figured my mom was like the fairy godmother in the story and I was so worried that she would get sick, too, just like in the story."

Sam swallowed and looked down at the book. Brooke reached out and squeezed her hand, which seemed to help Sam, and she continued. "But my mom said that when we planned the party, we were going to get help from other people *before* the party, so everything wouldn't go wrong on the day of the party."

"We will get help," Cole said.

"I bet there are lots of people who will help," Brooke agreed.

Sam nodded and smiled, a peaceful bliss on her face, and turned to the next page. "And at the party, all the dukes and duchesses showed up in their fanciest clothes, and Princess Samantha wore her favorite dress. It was a big fluffy one, and she wore shimmering ribbons in her hair and sparkly shoes."

Brooke sat up straighter. "I'll design your dress."

Samantha's eyes flew to Brooke's, disbelief and hopefulness on her face.

"I can make a dress that's perfect for you," Brooke repeated.

"I've known you a long time," Cole said, "and I can tell that you're stressed right now and probably have a lot on your plate. You don't have to do this, Brooke."

"No, I can do it. It's perfect timing."

"You're going to make me my very own By the Brooke dress?" Sam whispered, awe-struck. "For me?"

Brooke smiled and nodded, and Sam burst out of her chair and threw her arms around Brooke. "I love you, Brooke! You're the best fairy godmother ever!"

Shock and surprise washed over Brooke's face, and then she returned the hug, letting out a laughing breath. "As your dad said, you're a cool girl, Samster. I'd be honored to design you a dress."

When Cole had finally been able to picture himself with someone again after Amanda, this is exactly who he had pictured. Someone whose heart he was so drawn to. Someone who would bring this kind of joy to his daughter.

At the time Brooke had first walked into their lives, he'd seriously considered pursuing her. But he soon realized he couldn't. She was gone all the time, sometimes with only a few hours' notice. It hadn't mattered how attracted to her that he was— he had his daughter to think about, not just himself, and she deserved someone to be around for her. Plus, he craved stability in his life and he'd never get that with Brooke.

"Let's take a look at that list," Cole said as Sam climbed back into her seat. He needed to get his mind focused on something other than Brooke, or the attraction he felt toward her was going to rear up too strongly. "If we are going to get help from people before the party, we better get thinking about who we're going to ask."

Together they brainstormed people who could help with each item on the list. They had come up with a lot of names of people in town who could help with different parts, but there were still several items on the list that didn't have names next to them. As they made a plan for each item, the excitement level in the room grew. Cole had started off the evening feeling like this party was so outside of his comfort zone that it would be impossible to pull off, and now he couldn't wait to get started.

"Okay," Sam said, kneeling on her chair, her elbows on the table, leaning forward to read the list. "We still have decorations and activities with no one's names by them."

Brooke's eyes met Cole's and she opened her mouth like she was going to say something, then hesitated. Then she looked at Samantha and said, "Let's put our names by them. I think we can come up with some pretty good ideas."

"Really?" both Cole and Sam said at the same time.

Brooke looked as surprised at her offer to help as Cole was.

"Yes," Brooke said. "We're going to give you the perfect party, Princess Samantha."

As they walked toward the door to leave, Sam was between Cole and Brooke, and she wrapped an arm around both of them and squeezed them tight. "Thank you both for being my fairy godmothers, and for helping me plan a party that all the kids are going to love. The princess in the book didn't feel loved until the very end, but I feel loved right now."

He was so grateful that Brooke offered to help plan this party because she'd been right— it wasn't something he could've pulled off on his own. But right now, the part of him that had fallen for Brooke long ago warred with the disciplined part of him that worried about how much more difficult spending so much time with Brooke was going to make things. For both Sam and him.

BROOKE

"You volunteered for *what?*" Delbrina said, disbelief coloring every word.

Noemi turned away from the computer where they were uploading images to their online store and threw her arms up. "How are you going to have time for that and still prepare for Van Zandt?"

"I don't know," Brooke said. She'd shown up for work at six a.m. again this morning to start work on dealing with some issues her accountant had sent her, but she had found her mind wandering to Sam's party and very much against her will, to Cole. And in not a just-friends way.

They had kissed once before, but that had been a mistake. A fluke. Or at least that's what she had told herself. The feelings she started having last night, and the thoughts she was still having, felt very much not a fluke. Eventually this morning, she had given up on accounting and started working on designing Sam's dress before the others came in to work.

Now she was even more behind on the day. She shook her head. "Especially because Sam's birthday is only three days after returning from presenting to Van Zandt, so most of the preparations for her party will need to happen at the same time I'm preparing for the presentation."

Delbrina looked heavenward, shaking her head. Noemi, for all of her softness, stood tall, a fist on her hip, looking like a mother about to scold a child.

"For the record," Brooke said, "I had planned to not volunteer for anything. I was just there to help them come up with a plan and a list of people to ask. I'm very good at saying no." She hadn't always been good at it, but she had learned quickly. She couldn't have built a business the size of By the Brooke by getting distracted by things that didn't fit with her goals.

"But you weren't there. Samantha lost her mom, and the two of them had been planning to have this party for as long as Sam can remember. As we talked, Sam was just so happy and so excited, and it was contagious.

"When I was her age, I was the lead in my elementary school's play, and I had a grand idea of a cast party after the final show. My parents were both busy, and although they had always been civil to each other after the divorce, they didn't like each other a whole lot. But they still came together and made the day special for me and the whole cast."

Brooke shrugged. "I guess I just wanted Sam to have that moment, too. In the end, I decided I didn't want to say no this time."

Delbrina shook her head back and forth slowly. "You have a weakness for that girl. Always have."

Noemi's hands flew to her mouth and she gasped. Then, pointing at Brooke, she said, "And you've got a weakness for her dad!" She turned to look at Delbrina, still pointing at Brooke, as if the evidence was written across Brooke's face.

Was that heat rising in her cheeks? She really hoped she wasn't blushing.

A slow smile spread across Delbrina's face. "Brooke! When did this happen?"

"It *didn't* happen. My goodness, you two are quick to jump to conclusions. Okay, I'll admit that there was a moment when I felt a slight something," she continued a little louder to speak over Noemi's squeal, "but it lasted like thirty seconds, then I squashed it flat. Straying beyond friends with Cole is dangerous. And you know I'm not okay with *ever* dating someone from Nestled Hollow."

Brooke walked over to the rack room and rolled out the one with the clothing that they were going to show to

Van Zandt, "Besides, Back Porch Grill is my favorite place to eat in the country. If I dated its owner, then not only would I lose my best friend, but the awkwardness after we broke up would make me lose the ability to eat at the best restaurant anywhere."

Delbrina and Noemi both folded their arms and turned toward each other. "She doesn't want to date someone because of her stomach," Noemi said.

They both chuckled, then Delbrina said, "You know, though, it sounds reasonable. I wouldn't let anything get between me and that ice cream shop down the street."

Brooke inspected the rack with the clothing they needed to photograph for the lookbook.

"In all seriousness, though," Delbrina said, "knowing your weakness for that man and his daughter, you probably shouldn't have offered to have the planning meeting with them in the first place."

"Maybe," Brooke said, "but if I hadn't, I wouldn't have known that Sam needed a fancy party dress fit for a princess, and I wouldn't have come up with this." She pulled the giant sketchbook from its shelf and laid it on the table, and then flipped open to the page where she'd drawn a dress that was worthy of both royalty and her favorite nine-year-old.

"Oh, honey," Noemi breathed, a hand pressed over her heart. "That is breathtaking."

Delbrina reached a hand partway toward it. "Well, if

that isn't as fine as a frog's hair split four ways, I don't know what is."

Brooke smiled as she watched her team fawning over her creation. The truth was, she'd designed dresses for Samantha in her head plenty of times, just like she did with every person she met. Since Sam was so young, so the dress had changed over the years as Sam changed.

The design she sketched this morning, though, had come to her in a flash last night when the girl had turned to the page where the princess was all dressed up. Instantly, she had known that it was the perfect dress to use for Van Zandt's requirement to design something outside of what they normally did.

"This is it," Noemi said. "It's perfect."

Brooke and her team spent the rest of the day turning her sketch into a detailed pattern with notes, and then a muslin pattern on a dress form Brooke had adjusted to be what she was sure was Sam's size. It was a very detailed, ambitious pattern with a fitted bodice and a big fluffy skirt that went nearly to the ground, so it took a lot of sewing, then altering, then re-sewing, and then making more adjustments to get it just right.

She glanced down at her watch. "Are you two good to start taking this apart and turning it into a pattern while I'm at the Main Street Business Alliance meeting?"

"You've got it," Delbrina said around a mouthful of pins.

With as much as she had to do still, Brooke wasn't sure she should be going to the meeting at all. But she had been so hyper-focused on the dress all day, working at such a feverish pace, that she needed the two minutes of fresh air she got by walking to the meeting, along with the chance to flop down in a chair and do something different for a bit. Besides, Brooke had never missed a Business Alliance meeting that she had been in town for. No one missed them.

After opening the door to the basement of the library, she immediately spotted Cole chatting with Nate. Based on the animated smile on Cole's face, he was probably asking Nate if he would help to make the lift to the slide for the party. Nate looked rather amused at either Cole's description or his excitement. Hopefully, that meant he'd say yes to the project.

She found Whitney in her normal spot on the front row, wearing a blazer and a *Step away from the caps lock* t-shirt, and she sat down next to her friend. Whitney glanced at her and said, "You doing okay?"

Brooke suddenly realized she hadn't even glanced in a mirror since she got ready to go to work in the 5:00 hour this morning. "Why? How bad is it?"

"You've just got a little bit of an Einstein look going on."

"Einstein?" Brooke raised an eyebrow, but immediately

ran her fingers through her hair and hopefully tamed any hairs headed in crazy directions.

"You know. A wild excitement in the eyes. Like you just discovered the link between mass and energy."

"I discovered I need a massive amount of energy to make it through my next few days. Does that count?"

Cole slipped into the seat on her other side and leaned in and said, "Nate's in."

"That's fantastic!" Brooke said just as Ed and Linda Keetch got up to start the meeting. She tried to focus just as intently on the older couple as she had on Sam's dress, mostly to keep her focus from drifting to how great Cole smelled. He had spent all day working in a hot kitchen. How did he always smell like sandalwood, ginger, and citrus shampoo?

It was *not* intoxicating.

In fact, it wasn't even attractive.

He was a friend *only*.

She mentally shook a fist at Delbrina and Noemi for even bringing up her moment of misplaced attraction the day before and making it real with words, instead of just letting it be something ephemeral inside her head. If they hadn't, she probably wouldn't have even thought about it again.

Ed Keetch hooked his thumbs in his pockets and said, "I'm sure most of you are feeling in your pocketbooks the boost we got from skiers with all the snow this winter, but it sounds like we aren't quite up to where we need to be."

"But," Linda said, "we're hoping this spring will get us all in the black and give an extra boost to Nestled Hollow. We've got the Take Flight Festival in just a week, and that should help bring in quite a few tourism dollars."

After they discussed all the details of the festival, Ed leaned against the table behind him, one arm resting on it. "You've all done a mighty fine job of meeting the needs of everyone in Nestled Hollow, but I know we can all use some outside money coming in. I want you all to take a few minutes and brainstorm with the business owner beside you on ways you can bring people outside Nestled Hollow into your place of business."

Brooke immediately turned to Whitney. She put a hand on Cole's knee, and said, "Cole and I have a question to ask you."

Whitney's eyes shifted to Brooke's hand, and Brooke realized how much the action paired with the question made them seem like a couple. She pulled her hand back as quickly as she could. "Do you think your presses could print fancy invitations?"

Whitney paused, like she working the machines in her head. "I'm sure they could. Why? What do you have in mind?"

Brooke turned and met Cole's grin, then said to

Whitney, "Some very special party invitations for a very sweet little girl."

"Of course! I love Sam. I have some suppliers with fancy paper."

"One of my weekend waitresses, Halle, is going to school to be a graphic designer, and she's agreed to work with Sam to come up with something worthy of 'Princess Samantha's Perfect Party.'"

"But more on topic," Brooke said, giving a nod to Ed Keetch, "if you could get a website set up where people can design invitations, you could probably bring in customers throughout the county."

"That might be a possibility," Whitney said, tapping her finger on her lips. "I'm going to have to think on that some more."

Macie, the owner of Paws & Relax, grabbed the chair on the other side of Cole and brought it around to the front so she was facing the three of them. "Brooke, you know that dress that you made with me in mind that I wore to the Winter Formal at NHH? That dress was perfect. I don't even know myself well enough to have known that would be the most right dress possible, yet you did. That's a gift people would pay a lot of money for."

"She's right," Whitney said. "You can read a person's deepest emotions just by looking at them. You're brilliant at knowing what they want."

Cole nodded. "There are some rich people out there. I

bet some would be willing to fly here just to meet with you and have you design them a dress."

"True," Brooke said. That sounded just like something her mother would do. Truth be told, her dad would too—he'd been known to fly out of the country to be fitted for a suit by someone who was an expert in the field.

"There are plenty of people who need fancy dresses out there," Cole said. "Like people who present at the Oscars and those other awards shows on TV, and I don't know, fancy galas and things like that. If you could get your name out there, wealthy people would travel here to have you work your magic, because you're the best there is."

Her eyes widened. He thought she was the best? Not that he knew anything about the world of design, so it wasn't an objective assessment. But still, he thought about her that way?

Cole must've caught the moment of disbelief on her face, though, because he added, "I'm not sure you fully realize how incredible you are."

Brooke's breath caught in her throat and warmth spread in her chest at his words. She had been told many times that she was talented, by people in the industry who knew what they were talking about. But none of them had ever said it with the heart that Cole had.

———

Brooke picked up her phone when she saw the screen light up. It was a text from Cole.

> Cole: I stopped by the restaurant to help Hani close up and saw your car in the lot. Still working?

> Brooke: Yep. Big project. I think I've spent a few thousand calories today just on brainpower because I'm about ready to raid the mini-fridge.

> Brooke: Ketchup packets spread on week-old bagels can count as brain food, right?

She really needed to go shopping and bring some food to the office. She had been working far too many hours lately to have so little food around. She looked in the cupboard where there were occasionally some granola bars, but it was bare.

> Cole: PUT DOWN THE BAGELS

> Cole: Seriously, Brooke.

> Cole: The ketchup packets, too.

> Cole: I'm making food for you right now. Come over.

Brooke looked at the clock on her phone. It was a few minutes past ten, so the restaurant was closed. Sam must be having her weekly sleepover at her grandma's tonight. Her first thought was to tell him that he didn't have to make her food this late at night, especially when he was trying to close up the restaurant, but she was starving, and the ketchup packets weren't looking appetizing. So she closed up the office and headed over to the restaurant.

Cole unlocked the front door when he saw her through the glass, and she walked into the empty eating area and he locked it behind her.

"Choose a table," Cole said, "and I'll be right back with food."

Brooke took a seat at a table for two in the middle of the dining room as Cole headed to the kitchen. Hani must have been finishing up some things in the back because she heard him telling Cole goodbye not long after.

Cole emerged from the kitchen, holding two steaming plates of stir-fried vegetables and chicken over rice, and set both of them down on the table, the bigger one in front of her, then he grabbed two glasses of water he'd already filled from the bar and set them on the table. Her stomach hadn't seemed to realize exactly how hungry it was until she smelled the food, and it started growling loud enough for both of them to hear.

"Cole, it's been less than ten minutes since I texted! How do you work this kind of magic?"

He shrugged. "The veggies were already cut, the chicken and rice already cooked. I just threw them together. It wasn't a big deal. I can't turn on the lights up here, though, or people will think we're open." He turned on his cell phone flashlight on and laid it on the table. "I don't have any candles, either, so this will have to do."

"We can do one better than that." Brooke picked up his phone, went into his Netflix app, and searched for *fireplace*. She chose one of the videos of a fire burning in a fireplace and set it back on the table, grinning.

Cole raised an eyebrow, impressed. "Next best thing."

She took a bite of the delicious, warm meal and closed her eyes, savoring it. Then she pointed her fork at Cole. "You, Cole Iverson, are my very favorite thing about Nestled Hollow."

He laughed and took a bite of his food.

She glanced at her watch. "You're up past your bedtime. *And* you're eating past the window of time you consider it okay to eat dinner."

"Clearly, you're a bad influence on me."

Brooke had spent way too much of the day with her brain on work to talk about it any longer, so in an effort to keep the conversation away from it, she asked, "Is Sam excited about her party?"

Cole smiled. "It's all she talks about. Apparently, she's had this dream for years, and it's finally coming true." He paused a moment. "When you were a kid, did you have a favorite book like Sam did?"

"Absolutely." She took a swallow of water. "I think the book was called *You Know Someone Loves You*. Each page said something about the ways people show love, like 'You know someone loves you when they give you half their treat,' or 'You know someone loves you when they keep you company when you're sick,' or when they push you in a swing or pick a flower for you.

"But my favorite page of all was the one that said, 'when they bring you a balloon.' There was a girl on that page who was holding a red balloon that someone had given her, and her face was full of wonder and appreciation and happiness that I always stared at her expression and imagined feeling the same. I just knew she felt loved.

"And then the book ended with 'But most of all, you know someone loves you when they hold you in their arms all snug and tight, and tell you that they love you every night.' For a good year and a half, I didn't go to sleep without that book by my side, whether I was at my dad's house on one side of the country or my mom's on the other, or in a hotel anywhere in between. I loved that book like nothing else."

Brooke shook her head, chuckling. "It's been a long time since I've thought about that book. What about you?"

Cole nodded as he finished chewing his bite. "I don't

even remember what it was called, but I remember the picture on the cover perfectly. It was a story about a dragon who wanted to be a chef, so he made a kitchen in a clearing out of all the things he found in the woods. And as he was making a meal in his new kitchen, everybody came by to give him grief for it."

He paused a moment, looking off to the side like he was picturing it.

"You remember some of the words, don't you?" When he nodded, Brooke said, "Come on. You've got to tell me."

Cole exhaled. "I don't remember it all, but there was a part when the dragon first started preparing food that I can still remember, in the exact way my dad used to read it to me."

He cleared his throat and, using different voices, said, "'His momma said, 'Dragons swoop and they fly.' His daddy said, 'Dragons belong in the sky.' His best friend said, 'Dragons breathe fire and roar!' His sister said, 'They don't mix, measure, or pour.' But all of their doubtings, he simply ignored, while he chopped and he stirred and he spread and he poured. A pinch and a cup and a dollop and a squeeze, and then toasted it all with a flaming breeze.'

"And then of course at the end, his mom and his dad and his friend and his sister all wanted to eat the wonderful food he'd prepared. That book is what made me want to be a chef."

Brooke marveled at the man seated across from her,

his face glowing in the light of the fireplace on his phone in the middle of a restaurant he'd first dreamed of owning when he was a kid reading a book about a dragon.

"Yep," she said, loading another bite on her fork, "you're definitely my favorite part of Nestled Hollow."

Cole finished ladling the red pepper sauce on the two spicy tortellini dishes he was making, then put them on the pass-through counter and looked at the next ticket in the longest line of tickets he'd had in a very long time. He took an extra second to glance at the lobby— people were *still* coming in. Brooke made her way through the throng of people waiting to be seated and met his eyes, a question in hers. One of these never-ending tickets was probably one she'd called in.

He nodded for her to come back, and then flipped over the steak strips he was grilling and looked at the next ticket.

He dropped a basket of fries into the fryer, grabbed a fish fillet, cut it into three strips, breaded it, and then dropped it into a different fryer basket before using the tongs to put a piece of chicken on the grill.

"Are you seriously alone back here?" Brooke said when she rounded the corner into the kitchen.

"Yep." He tossed some onions, mushrooms, and peppers in with the steak on the grill. "Ann was supposed to work the twelve to eight shift, but she's violently ill, and so is Hani, who's supposed to work the dinner shift."

He cut open a hoagie bun, buttered it, and put it on the bread grill, then glanced again at the tickets and put seven hamburger patties on the grill.

"Lori already worked the opening shift and her kid has a dance performance tonight. I even called Bill—he'll come out of retirement if I'm in a tight spot, but he's away visiting grandkids. So of course that's when a tour bus comes into town."

"*Two* tour buses. I saw them parked in the dirt lot past Main. Joey's and Keetch's are just as packed."

Cole groaned, turned over the steak and vegetables, drizzled on the sauce, then put two slices of cheese on top. "I dusted off the simplified menus, so everyone only has seven items to choose from, and they're ones low on prep. Still, though, this crowd is insane." He put the steak and everything on the bun and plated it, then pulled up the basket of fries and the basket with the fish, and added fries to the steak and everything plate.

"You need help."

"Clearly. I even tried calling in a couple of my wait staff, but everyone who isn't here is sick. But I'll be okay."

Brooke was quiet for a moment. He glanced in her direction as she put her phone on the back table and put on an apron. Then she was pulling that beautiful brown hair back and wrapping a band around it that he swore had appeared out of nowhere. She was washing her hands when he said, "Brooke, you don't know how to cook."

"True. I probably wouldn't be alive if it weren't for you feeding me. But I take direction well."

He paused a moment, wondering if she even had time to be here, but then decided he couldn't turn down any offer to help on a day like today. "Okay, watch me make these fish tacos because there's half a dozen more of them on the current tickets."

As a friend, Brooke leaned in much closer than an employee ever would as he demonstrated how to put together the tacos. And he was certain that he'd never had an employee before who smelled as good as she did.

"Got it," she said. "Tortillas, coleslaw, avocado, pico, queso fresco, limes on the side. Want me to make them now?"

Cole put them on the pass-through counter with their ticket, and said, "Not yet. See that sourdough bread over there? Cut three slices about half an inch thick, spread that garlic butter over there on them, then put them butter side down on that bread grill. Then dish up three bowls of tomato basil soup. When the bread's done, place it butter side up in the bowl."

He had trained employees dozens of times over the years but never had he trained them on a day like today, and at first, it seemed to take just as long to explain what to do as it would've been to do it himself. And Brooke, for as confident as she seemed in virtually any situation, was getting flustered at every mistake she made or thing she didn't know how to do.

"Wait, you can't pull the ticket until we have all the items made on it. That one still needs a stuffed baked potato."

"Right," Brooke said, whirling in one direction and then the other.

"Potatoes are warming in the oven," Cole directed. The nice thing about training Brooke was that she had eaten practically every item on his menu, so she at least had a general idea of how it was supposed to look. "And the pulled pork is in that warmer. Sauces are beside it. Green onions and shredded cheese are over here."

As Cole cut, breaded, and dropped into the fryer enough fish to feed half a football team, Brooke worked behind him. "Doing okay?" he asked. "There are a lot of frustrated grunts coming from your side of the kitchen."

"This potato is fighting me." She turned and flashed him a grin. "But don't worry, I'm going to win. If you had any music playing back here, you wouldn't hear my frustrated grunts."

"We also wouldn't hear the things we need to say to each other." He put three more sets of beef strips on the grill and chopped them with the spatula to separate the meats. "The kitchen is all about communication."

Brooke brought the plate with the baked potato to the counter next to the grill and sat it down next to him. "Well, I'm going to communicate to you right now that people work better to music." She reached out for the green onions at the same time he reached for the sliced onions, and their hands bumped, and for the first time in the kitchen since Amanda died, Cole felt a charged heat race through him at the accidental touch.

Brooke batted his hand out of the way. "Guests first."

She sprinkled the green onions on the stuffed potato then turned to face him, her hip resting against the counter, while he grabbed the sliced onions and put some on each pile of beef. "If you're not going to have the professionals provide the music, then we'll have to provide it as amateurs." She turned and placed the baked potato on the pass-through counter, put the ticket under the edge of the plate, then said, "Hmm...what's a food song..."

Then, as she got out two salad bowls for the next order and filled them with romaine, she started belting out the chorus to "American Pie." She had a great singing voice.

He didn't know why that surprised him— everything about her seemed polished. "Come on, Cole, sing."

"I don't sing."

"You're supposed to humor the volunteer help."

He grunted. Then he took a deep breath, knowing that he might as well stop fighting because she would eventually talk him into it. He sang the next line of the chorus. If he was going to sing, he figured he might as well do it right, so he belted it out too, as he moved two pieces of chicken to the cutting board and started slicing them.

Brooke put the tomatoes and corn and black bean salsa on the salads as they sang the last two lines together. She sprinkled the shredded cheese on the two salads and drizzled them with honey-lime vinaigrette, and he finished them off with the sliced chicken and a flourish as he held out the last note.

Cole laughed out loud. It never ceased to amaze him the kinds of things Brooke could get him to do that he never even thought he'd do.

She put the salads on the counter and placed the ticket just under the edge. "See what music does for you? What's next?"

As they continued to work, Brooke humming when she wasn't singing out loud, they started to get more in sync with each other. The tickets kept coming in fast, but they were keeping up with them better than he'd have guessed they would.

It didn't take long to get into a rhythm. She still made little newbie mistakes that made him chuckle, like not taking care of the tickets in the right order, or not knowing how to cook the pasta correctly, but he liked being in the kitchen with her. It fit. She fit.

"Why don't you advertise outside of Nestled Hollow?"

Cole turned over the hamburgers, chicken, and steak he had on the grill, then shrugged.

"Maybe it's time you did," Brooke said, bringing the plate with the stuffed potato over to the counter next to him to sprinkle on the green onions. "You're an incredibly talented chef, Cole. You could get the extra business easy."

He tried to keep the smile from crossing his face. "So I can have more busy nights like this?"

"Exactly." She sliced more bread for the soup, and then started singing the chorus to "Firework."

Maybe it wasn't such a bad thing that he had been left with no help on such a busy night.

He put meat on the grill for four more steak and everything sandwiches, and then realized he was going to need more green peppers. He turned toward the walk-in and bumped right into Brooke as she headed toward the bread grill. They both froze for a moment, chest to chest, barely an inch apart, and Cole was struck, once again, by how beautiful she was. He was as experienced dowsing his feelings for Brooke as he was at making a flawless soufflé, but just like with a soufflé that fell even when you thought you did everything right, the heat of those feelings resurfaced like someone fired up a blowtorch.

He wanted to get married again, for his sake and Sam's. And so he wouldn't have to break his promise to Amanda. But he didn't know how he'd ever be able to move past Brooke. He was no longer sure he even wanted to. Being around her made him happy, and he liked who he was with her in his life.

They both attempted to move out of the other's way but stepped in the same direction. Instead of giving the standard "would you like to dance" comment, without a word, Brooke grabbed his hand with hers, lifted it high, and then she spun around in a circle before dropping his hand and curtseying. He couldn't help the smile that spread across his face as he gave her a bow.

While he walked toward the fridge, she said, "Do you realize that after nearly three years of friendship, that's the most dancing we've ever done?"

"It's a travesty," he said before pulling open the door and walking inside to get the sliced green peppers. He stopped inside the walk-in and closed his eyes, breathing the cool air in slowly and out slowly, trying to put out that fire of attraction and reclaim his ability to dowse feelings for Brooke.

It can't work, he reminded himself.

He took another small moment to fix that in his mind, and then he grabbed the green peppers and headed back into the kitchen and the long list of tickets that awaited him. "Are you in town for a bit?"

She nodded. "My next trip isn't for a week."

"Do you know what's as fun as dancing?" he asked as he got back to the steak and everythings. "Painting." He turned to see Brooke's confused face. "Nate says he's had more fun working on the lift for Sam's party than he has building anything in a long time, so he expects to be done by late tomorrow night. Are you up for a painting party in two days?"

"Oh, wow! That's fantastic! Um, yes. Of course, I'll be there."

He didn't miss the hesitation in her voice, though. Brooke was normally excited about things like this, and he wondered what could be holding her back.

BROOKE

Brooke ladled up bowls of soup and wondered why she had ever said yes to a night of painting when she had so much going on. She had gotten so caught up in the rhythm of the kitchen— once she finally got the rhythm— that work hadn't even crossed her mind.

Once she got the basics of helping with this smaller menu, she got in the flow of making each plate, each one an individual creation that went from start to finish within a couple of minutes. The sense of fulfillment from finishing things and clearing a ticket and sending food off to hungry stomachs was intoxicating. And, actually, rather fun. For the first time, she truly understood why Cole loved what he did so much.

Since he brought up something that would demand her time, though, everything she needed to do and everything she currently should be doing raced through her head like they were tumble-running down a hill.

And the list of the items that she wasn't going to be able to get done today because she'd spent more than two hours here was growing by the second. Maybe she could cancel painting with him. It was the wisest choice. She couldn't exactly make a clone of herself, and there was simply more to do than what would fit in the time she had.

Staying focused meant saying no to things she wanted to do but didn't fit with her vision. Growing her business and taking advantage of opportunities, especially ones as big as a possibility with Van Zandt, had been part of her vision since the beginning.

Cole looked at the tickets, seeming to count the number of burgers he needed to put on the grill, then ducked down to look through the pass-through, and waved at someone. Brooke leaned back from where she worked on preparing four plates of fish tacos and saw Roger Havrilo contemplating the texture on the table in front of him.

Cole chuckled. "Whenever an order for a medium-well burger, pickles only comes in, I know that Roger's here."

Brooke reached for the onions, and Cole leaned over and grabbed her wrist. "Pico next. No onions." She shook her head. She knew that.

"You okay?"

She flashed him a smile. "Yep." *Focus, Brooke.*

Cole put the burger on the bun with only pickles and added fries to the plate. "Roger's been struggling ever since his dog died. I'm going to take this out to him. Will you keep an eye on things for me?" Five plates with buns sat next to the grill, and Cole pointed to each one in succession. "Medium, medium-rare, well, well, medium-well. This one has no tomatoes, and this one no mayo. Got it?"

Brooke nodded and repeated back what Cole had just said, then he took Roger's plate and headed out to the lobby.

As she dressed the buns, Brooke started thinking about the lookbooks she needed to take to her presentation. Delbrina had let the designer know about their new timeline, but it suddenly occurred to her that she wasn't sure if that meant she'd also let the photographer know. The designer couldn't do much without the photos. And she needed to check to make sure that all the items for the book were ready for the photographer.

"Wait, no," she said out loud. "This one doesn't have mayo." She switched plates with the last one since she hadn't gotten to it yet. Which one was without tomato again? Was it the second or the third?

She glanced at the grill, then jerked her hand forward, grabbed the spatula, and turned over one of the patties.

She normally ordered her burgers medium, and the cooked side looked the way she liked it. Maybe if she didn't leave it long on this side, it could work as medium-rare. She had no idea.

One was supposed to be medium, though, right? She flipped a second burger and tried to remember. How did she know when one was medium-well or well?

And oh! They weren't the only thing on the grill! She flipped over the steak strips for two sandwiches and then turned the three chicken breasts. "Buns, buns," she said as she grabbed two hoagie buns and sliced them down the middle, buttered them, then put them on the bun grill.

The chicken must be for salads, and she hadn't even started them. She ran to the prep station and pulled out three salad bowls and started putting in the lettuce.

Sam's dress pattern was coming right along, but some tweaks needed to be made before cutting out the actual fabric and sewing it.

She let out a choked sound when she realized she'd probably left the burgers too long, and ran to the grill. That was definitely not medium-rare. Maybe that could be the medium-well one, and she could put on a new medium-rare patty. She peeked under the medium one and tried to guess if it could still count as medium. She put a slice of cheese on both of them, like she'd seen Cole do, then reached for the bottom buns on the plate. Which ones went to which plates again?

Putting her fingertips on the bun, she scooped the patty up with the spatula and went to put it on its top bun, then realized she never finished dressing them. But she needed this burger to stop cooking. She hovered the spatula between the plate and the grill, and then left the patty on the spatula and put it on the side of the grill, leaning up a bit, hoping it wouldn't fall off.

The steaks were done, and she hadn't even added the veggies. She threw some on the grill and then went to the buns, having no clue which one wasn't supposed to have tomatoes. Cole had been gone for less than five minutes, and everything had already turned to chaos.

"Thank you, Brooke," Cole said as he walked back into the kitchen. "He really needed that. Are you okay? You look a little flustered."

She nodded and stepped back, letting Cole survey the damage. With an uncanny calmness, he finished dressing the buns, started a new burger, got all the other burgers plated, along with the two steak and everythings, finished the salads and topped them with the chicken he just sliced, and got all the plates in the pass-through with their corresponding tickets tucked underneath.

She had gotten so far out of the groove of the kitchen that she couldn't seem to just jump back in without causing more chaos. So she just watched Cole work for a moment. No motions were wasted— he moved with grace and efficiency like he instinctively knew what needed to happen in precisely what order. It was mesmerizing to watch him in his element.

She admired his calmness— his ability to be at peace, knowing he was doing exactly what he should be doing. He even seemed to know that stopping for a moment to go comfort someone in need, even with so many tickets waiting, was exactly what he was supposed to be doing. Cole may schedule his life to a near-obsessive amount, but he also scheduled in people. It was that quality that always drew her to people. It was the thing that had drawn her to Cole when she'd first moved to Nestled Hollow.

And suddenly she realized that her admiration of Cole had crossed from friendship into something more. Why had that been happening so often lately?

She stepped up to the line of tickets, trying to figure out what to do next. Her head was a swirling mess of confusing feelings for her friend and all the lists of things she needed to do for work. Adding to the items on these tickets was throwing a bowling ball at her mental list, scattering all the pins.

She glanced through the window at Roger. The pensive look he'd had before was gone and his whole demeanor had brightened. Cole found a way to schedule people even during his busiest times. She could help him paint the lift for Sam's party and still find a way to get things done. People mattered.

Just like with everything else, this was a mind game,

and she always won mind games. She went through the items for work that were at the front of her mind and decided when she was going to work on each of the items so her brain could relax and know that everything was going to be taken care of. Right now she was in the kitchen of Back Porch Grill, working alongside one of her favorite people, and that was where her mind needed to be.

Cole started humming and she smiled, knowing that he wouldn't be humming if she hadn't brought some music to his kitchen. The rhythm and energy she had felt before returned, and she started making three stuffed potatoes and knew that this time she would win, not them.

"Brooke!"

Her head jerked up at the sound of her name, and she looked through the pass-through to see who had called it out. Noemi stood at the bar directly in front of the window, panic on her face.

"Your mom is here!"

"Here?" Brooke asked. "In Nestled Hollow?"

"Yes! She said she's been texting you about meeting for dinner and you haven't responded, but she knew that you were in town. She stopped into the store to look for you. Delbrina's stalling her, but she'll be over here any minute."

Brooke's eyes shifted across the lobby to the door as her mom walked inside. She only glanced around for a moment before meeting Brooke's eyes.

Brooke turned around, her hand on the ties of her apron, hesitating.

"Go," Cole said. "I've got this just fine. Look— the lobby is clearing out, so the tour buses must be taking off soon. Don't keep Rose waiting. There's a table for you two, and don't worry, I'll make your mom something special."

She put her hand on his arm. "Thank you, Cole."

As she tore off her apron, brushed her hands down her shirt, and then ran to the sink, he said, "I'm pretty sure I'm the one needing to do the thanking."

She was about to say, "That's what friends are for," but the word "friends" suddenly felt strange. Not quite right. She washed her hands and her arms up to the elbows to get rid of the smell of cooking but realized she was probably just replacing it with the smell of antiseptic soap.

As she headed out toward the lobby, she glanced down at her phone. Seventeen missed texts and four missed phone calls. *Oops.*

"Mom," Brooke said as she met her mom in the lobby, arms outstretched. She gave her mom a quick hug, as usual making sure that she didn't touch her mother's hair so it wouldn't get messed up. "This is an unexpected surprise."

"Well, I *tried* to make it less unexpected."

"I know." Brooke held her phone up, evidence that she was now being responsible and had it with her.

"I can seat you right over here," Ryleigh said, and

seated them in a booth, setting silverware rolled in a napkin in front of each of them.

"No need for menus," Brooke said, then, in answer to her mom's questioning look, said, "Cole is going to make us something special."

"That sounds lovely."

Rose examined Brooke, or at least all that she could see from behind the table, and Brooke resisted the urge to look down to see how often her apron had failed her. She also resisted the urge to reach up and pull out the band holding her ponytail when her mom's gaze landed there but managed to keep her posture strong and confident.

"What were you doing back in the kitchen? Delbrina wouldn't say, but I got the impression that you had been here for a while."

Brooke smiled at Dex as he set a glass of water in front of each of them and announced that he would be their waiter for the evening. "Would you like anything to drink?"

After more than two hours in the kitchen, Brooke was ready to drain her water cup and start on a second, but she just said, "Water is good for me," and took a sip.

"Club soda, please," her mom said.

As soon as Dex left, Brooke answered her mom's question. "I was just helping out a friend."

"Right now."

It was more a statement than a question, but still, Brooke nodded, then took a sip of her water.

Her mom clasped her hands, resting them on the edge of the table, and let out a long slow breath. Rose McClellan, businesswoman extraordinaire, had shown up to this dinner. "What Van Zandt expects of you is a *lot*."

"I know."

"You're an immensely talented girl, Brooke. But talent alone isn't going to get you this. They want to know that you can run a business."

She also knew this. If they only cared about her designs, they could've checked out all of the thirty-six people that were originally in the running without any of them knowing they were being considered.

"What's the McClellan family motto?"

Brooke smiled at her mom. "Are you going to make me repeat it?"

"Yes." She smiled back at Brooke, and Rose McClellan, Brooke's mom, broke through. "You're thirty-two now. I don't get to assert my motherly authority very often anymore. Humor me."

"Decide what opportunities you want, then put yourself in their path and grab hold when one comes by."

Her mom nodded once, a satisfied look on her face. "Brooke, you decided that you wanted your designs at Van Zandt's a long time ago. You put yourself in their path, and a huge opportunity has come by. You saw how much

Van Zandt did for my cosmetics career—it would've taken me a couple of decades to launch my career as far as they took it in three short years. You need to grab hold with both hands."

Brooke opened her mouth to tell her mom about the progress she had made, but her mom held up a hand. "Now I know that friendships are important to you. I know this adorable town is important to you. But Brooke, there's one important thing you need to remember: you can work on friendships at any time. You can only prepare for your Van Zandt presentation— a once-in-a-lifetime opportunity— right now."

COLE

After returning from a hardware store in Mountain Springs, Cole and Sam carried the paint supplies and buckets of paint into the empty room to the side of Back Porch Grill's lobby.

Nate was wiping the last of the sawdust off his creation and when he saw them, he turned and said, "Well, what do you think?"

Sam raced forward and threw her arms out, attempting to wrap it in a hug.

Cole laughed. "You've got the Sam Seal of Approval." Then he walked around it, marveling at what Nate had created. It was octagonal and looked like a castle tower.

"Sam, come here. I want to demonstrate." Nate opened a two-foot-high door facing the front of the store. "Welcome to your lift to the top of the highest tower."

Sam, giddy with excitement, stepped into the little column recessed into the tower wall that was just her size.

"There's an electric motor in this thing. So you can wave to all of the dukes and duchesses, and when you're ready, this is the switch right here next to you. Just push the up button."

Sam made a show of waving her best princess wave at them and then pushed the button. As the platform raised her to the top of the tower, it slowly turned so that by the time she was at the top of the six-foot-high structure, she was facing the opposite direction, which put her facing the correct way to slide down to the "courtyard," just like the book showed. Sam squealed with delight and laughed as she slid down the slide.

When she landed on the floor, she ran to Nate. "In my book, it said that all the people came together to make the party magical and you made the most magical thing of all. It's even better than my imagination! And that's impressive because Mrs. Alvarez says I have a really good imagination."

"This," Cole said, shaking his head and motioning to it, unable to find the right words. "You did good work, Nate. This was much better than my imagination, too. If there's ever any way I can repay you—"

"Stop," Nate said. "This is me repaying you for all the times you brought my crew warm food on cold days. Besides," he put his hand on the side of the tower wall,

"I've had more fun building this than I have anything in a long time. If I had kids, I'd build them things like this all the time."

After he and Sam thanked him several more times and said goodbye, Sam crouched down by the cans of paint, looking at each one. "When's Brooke coming?"

Cole pulled out his phone, but Brooke hadn't responded to the text he sent letting her know that they were back with the paint. He sent her a quick *Are you still free to help us paint?*

Sam stood up. "Did she go out of town? Is she not coming?"

The sadness in his daughter's eyes made his chest hurt.

"She's in town, and don't you worry— she'll be here. She's just running behind." But he wasn't sure. He remembered the hesitation in her voice when he'd asked her to come. "What do you say we get started?"

He and Sam had watched YouTube videos the night before about painting techniques to make the walls look like stone, and he was excited to try it. He poured the medium gray paint into the tray and got them both rollers. He worked on painting the top half, and Sam rolled her paint on the bottom half.

When they were about one-third of the way finished with the base coat, Sam said, "Do you think something bad happened to Brooke?"

"I'm sure she's okay," Cole said. "Just busy." For most

of the time he'd known Brooke, he'd seen her as being flighty and unreliable. But somewhere along the way, he realized that he'd been wrong. She traveled more than anyone he'd ever known, but she was reliable. If she couldn't make it, she would've called and canceled.

Sam put her roller into the paint tray, loading it up with more paint. "Did she sound excited when you asked her to come? Because painting is pretty exciting. Did you tell her it was going to be exciting?"

"He did," Brooke said as she came into the room. "Sorry I'm late. I was working on your dress, and it was a really hard part where I needed eight hands and only had four."

"You had four hands?"

"Mine and Noemi's. Delbrina couldn't stay late. Wow! This looks amazing!"

When Sam finished showing the lift and the slide to Brooke and gave her a roller so she could help, too, Cole finally got a chance to talk with Brooke.

"I haven't seen you in a couple of days. What have you been up to?"

"Putting together a presentation for work."

Cole stopped painting and faced her. "This whole time? Why didn't you say anything? I would've brought you over some food. Who's been feeding you?"

Brooke laughed. "You are genuinely worried I would die of starvation, aren't you? Well, this time, my mother is responsible for keeping me alive. She was worried I wouldn't get the presentation done in time, so she had Elsmore Market bring me a stash of sandwiches, soups, veggie trays, and fruit trays to keep in my work fridge."

"Wow. That woman's a slave driver."

Brooke rolled the paint onto the next section. "Well, she didn't call Treanor's Outdoor Rentals to send over a cot to keep me from going home to sleep, so I'm calling it a win."

"Why does she want you to work so much?" Cole put down his roller and got out a paintbrush to get the top and bottom edges. "It's not like you work for her."

"She just doesn't want me to lose an opportunity I've been given."

"Is this to get your dresses into a boutique?"

"Something like that."

"What's my dress like?" Sam asked.

"I don't want to show you before it's finished, but I *really* can't wait to show you. It's a dress fit for a princess. A princess walking down a runway."

Sam looked dreamily up toward the ceiling. "I would love to walk down a runway in a beautiful dress." Then she looked at Brooke. "Have you ever had someone wearing one of your dresses walk down a runway?"

"Yep. A few times. It's fun."

He had known Brooke for nearly three years but hadn't known that. If he had to guess, he'd say that was a big deal, but Brooke just kept painting like it was nothing.

"Have *you* ever walked down a runway?"

Brooke shook her head. "The designers don't model their own clothes. Instead, there's this spot where you can peek out from behind the curtains backstage, and no one ever notices, but then you can see everyone's faces when they see the dresses you created."

"Like a spy." Sam grinned and held out a thumbs-up. Brooke shifted her roller to the other hand and held out a thumbs-up, too, and Sam touched her thumb to Brooke's.

Sam would give a hug to a porcupine if it looked like it needed it or if it showed her a kindness. But thumb bumps she reserved for only a select few who had worked their way into, as Sam put it, her deepest heart.

"Okay," Samantha said, "it's time for phase two."

Brooke met Cole's eyes and they shared a smile.

"Last night, me and my dad stayed up for a long time watching YouTube videos on how to make this paint look like it's stone."

Brooke raised an eyebrow at Cole, impressed, and he stood a little taller.

"The secret to turning paint into stone is..." Sam dragged out the word, then brought out the objects behind her back with a flourish. "Sponges!"

Sam handed one to Cole and one to Brooke then picked up a third one and dipped one side into the lighter gray paint. "You have to make sure you don't get too much paint on your sponge— the video said that was important. And then you touch it so so so lightly on the darker paint and voila! Look at that!" She touched the sponge to a few more places around the first. "It really looks like stone, doesn't it?"

The sponging went fairly quickly, and truthfully, it was turning out much better than he feared it would. Once they were done, Cole poured some of the paint from the quart of darker gray into two paper cups, and Sam brandished two thin brushes.

"Okay, here's the plan. Daddy, I want you to start right here at this edge of the lift and paint the lines that will make it look like it's big blocks of stone, instead of looking like it's one giant rock. You go around that side. Brooke, you start on this edge of the lift and go around this side. Go all the way to the top, and you can stop when you meet in the middle. A yardstick for you, and a yardstick for you so you can paint the stones straight. One foot high by two feet wide, please."

Cole chuckled, shook his head, and wondered again what his little girl was going to be like as an adult.

"I'm going to use this brush," she held up one a little thicker, "and start painting vines growing up the tower wall in the lift, just like the picture in the book. Deal?"

"Deal," he and Brooke both said.

As Sam took her cup of green paint into the column

for the lift, he and Brooke started painting the lines of stone mortar on the outside of the tower. He couldn't help glancing over at Brooke often— even wearing old jeans and one of his ancient flannel shirts that was a couple of sizes too big for her, she was beautiful. Her hair was pulled back in a high ponytail, enhancing her cheekbones and showing off the smear of paint she had on her temple.

He decided that one of his favorite things about her was that the expression on her face, whether it was resting, concentrating, serious, confused, amused, or anything in between, was happy. Like happiness was such a part of who she was that it couldn't help but come out.

Before long, he and Brooke were far enough around their own sides of the tower that they couldn't see each other and he could concentrate more on what he was doing. Sam was still hidden in her little cove, singing a song about Princess Samantha that she was making up as she went along. Eventually, though, he and Brooke rounded their corners enough that they could see each other. Or at least the parts of each other that weren't hidden by the slide that was between them.

They each painted the upper part of the tower first, then the bottom half, and worked their way under the slide. Side by side, they knelt under the slide, painting in its shadows, Sam singing her song on the other side of the tower in her little cubby.

"So," Cole said, "That presentation you're preparing. It's a big deal, isn't it?"

Brooke hesitated a moment like she wasn't sure she wanted to answer, but then she nodded.

"And you still have a lot to do."

Again she nodded. "Good guess."

"And yet you're here."

She met his eyes, searching his face. "Because here's important, too."

He searched her face, too, like it held all the answers to everything. To whether their friendship could also work out as a romantic relationship. If it would be what Sam needed. If it would be what he needed.

Brooke reached out a hand, seeming nervous and tentative, and brushed her fingertips on what he was sure was a paint smudge on his cheek. He reached up and touched his hand over the top of hers, and she responded by pressing her palm against his cheek.

He ran his fingertips down her hand, looking into those beautiful brown eyes of hers more deeply than he'd ever dared look before. In them, he saw kindness, grace, determination, and loyalty, and he wondered how he'd ever doubted whether they should be more than friends.

Paintbrush still in hand, Brooke leaned toward him, and like an invisible string formed from years of friendship was pulling them together, Cole mirrored her action.

As his eyes fluttered shut in the last moment before

they closed the remaining distance, Samantha said, "Hey Brooke, want to go to the Take Flight Festival with me?"

Brooke hit her head underneath of the slide as she hurried to turn and stand. "Sam. Hi. I, uh...what?"

Cole banged his knee against the wet paint as he exited their way-too-visible hideout under the slide, only slightly more gracefully than Brooke did.

Sam cocked her head to the side, confused. "Do you want to go to the Take Flight Festival?"

"Sure," Brooke said, still red-faced and flustered.

"I don't know, honey," Cole said. "Brooke has a big project to finish. Isn't Grandma taking you?" He looked to Brooke, to see if he could guess whether her answer was thought through and one she wouldn't regret later, or if it had simply been an answer thrown out in an attempt to make the situation less awkward.

"She's taking me to the kite festival in the afternoon, but when it turns into the parade on Main Street, she has to leave to go to her club in Mountain Springs. And you have to do the food. So I thought maybe Brooke..." Samantha folded her arms. "Why are you two acting weird?"

"Because," Brooke said, drawing out the word, "I just remembered that I have some important work emails I have to send before I can go home." She glanced at Cole. "And I was telling your dad that I feel terrible having to leave before helping clean everything up."

"And I told her not to feel bad because we're so grateful that she could come help." But all he could think about was how much he wished that their kiss hadn't been interrupted.

"I am, too," Samantha said. "Doesn't it look great? It's just like the castle tower in the book!"

The three of them stepped back and admired their work. They did do a pretty spectacular job.

Brooke leaned down, hugged Sam, and said goodbye. Then she looked back at Cole, a fingertip touching her lips and an expression on her face that he couldn't read. He wasn't sure if she was worried about the kiss after their last one had gone so wrong, or if she had been thinking about what it would've felt like to complete their kiss. Was she glad it was interrupted or sad?

He'd have given anything at that moment to know.

ten

Brooke kicked off her shoes and collapsed onto the couch in the social corner of her offices, Delbrina sitting down next to her with Noemi claiming a padded chair, all of them putting their feet on the coffee table. They had just spent a marathon morning with the photographer, photographing each piece for their lookbook.

Some of the pieces weren't finished yet, and Brooke had gone back to her office after painting and worked until two a.m. and met her staff back in the office at seven to continue.

As they prepared each piece for the photographer, as usual, many adjustments needed to be made as they went. And with their tight deadline, the photos had to be whisked off to the designer as they went. The designer said she'd have the final pages ready for her to approve within the hour, which meant they'd be able to get it sent to the printer in time to make their deadline.

She wished this trip to Los Angeles wasn't in the middle of everything. It was compressing their already impossibly small time frame.

"I hope you don't need me for a minute," Noemi said, "because I don't think this chair is planning to release me for the next six hours or so."

"I don't think I've ever been this tired," Delbrina said. "I don't know how you're still alive, girl, with all the hours you've been working."

"Are you sure I'm still alive?" Brooke held out her arm. "Check my pulse." She was pretty impressed that she was still able to function. And more than that, she was impressed at how well she'd been able to stay focused all morning, especially with as often as the almost-kiss with Cole had entered her mind.

She had kissed plenty of guys over the years. And she'd kissed Cole exactly one time over the years. Yet despite it going wrong before, last night's kiss that never happened made her realize that she wanted to kiss him more than she'd wanted to kiss anyone in a very long time. Possibly ever.

Why? What made her heart think this was okay? Did it not ever listen to her brain? That one time they had kissed, they both immediately knew it was wrong. And if she hadn't known on her own, Cole had made it pretty clear that night that they could never be an item. Besides, her brain had been saying plenty loud enough for years that she didn't want a long-term relationship.

And that she wasn't okay with having a short-term relationship with anyone in Nestled Hollow.

And that she didn't want to do anything to jeopardize a friendship that she really valued and enjoyed and very much relied on.

She knew that partnering as equals never worked out. Yet that day spent cooking and last night painting had worked out pretty well. Especially that part where they were painting under the slide.

Stop, she told herself. She knew that the more she thought about him, the harder it would be to resist the urge to turn their friendship into something more. She needed to distract herself.

But her brain was too tired to think about work, and she was too tired to get off this couch. Her stomach was growling for food pretty loudly, though. She focused on that. And on all the different foods she'd eat if only she could get up the energy to go get them.

Except for every food item she dreamed about made her think of Cole.

And how much she wanted that kiss.

"Noemi," she said, "channel my mother. Tell me how much I don't want a relationship."

Noemi sat up straighter in her chair and cleared her throat. "Now, Brooke," she said in a voice that was much too high, "Do you know what's important? It's not a husband, I'll tell you that. What's important is work." Then, in her normal voice, Noemi said, "I'm sorry—I can't pull that off with any conviction right now. We've worked too many hours and I can't tell you what I'd give right now to have a husband waiting at home to take care of me."

"I've got you," Delbrina said. Then in a low voice that must be her interpretation of Brooke's dad, she said, "You might think you get along well with a potential partner, but heed my advice: stay away. Because as soon as you form a partnership, badness happens."

"Badness?"

"It's the best I can do. With the schedule we've been keeping, my brain cells are too fried to come up with the fancy words your dad would use."

The bell on the front door of Best Dressed dinged and the three of them turned their heads a small fraction toward the sound.

"I know the sign says we're right in the middle of normal business hours," Noemi said, "but we really should've put up the closed sign."

"Agreed," Delbrina said.

Before Brooke managed to get up enough energy to so much as sit up straight, Cole appeared in the doorway between the retail store and the offices, and Brooke let out a sigh of relief that it wasn't a customer.

"Knock, knock."

"As long as you're not going to make me move an inch," Brooke said, "you can come in."

Cole was carrying a big paper bag and a cup holder with three drinks in it. He set both down on the coffee table, and then he took a seat in the empty padded chair. "All three of your cars were in the back lot when I left late last night, and they were there when I came in early this morning. So I figured you probably needed some sustenance right about now."

"You brought us food?" Noemi asked. "I love you, Cole. Will you be my husband?"

Cole chuckled and pulled three to-go containers out of the bag. "I figured you'd need a hearty meal, so I brought hand-pulled, slow-roasted turkey breast sandwiches on focaccia with avocados and sprouts. And because your brains might need a boost after all the abuse you've been giving them, I brought blueberry, beet, and banana smoothies."

"Oh my lands, that's so sweet I may cry," Delbrina said. "I'm going to tell this story to my man when I get home, see if it gives him any ideas."

Noemi and Delbrina sat up like normal people to eat, but Brooke couldn't do it. She'd put in more hours than they had by far, so she just reached her hands out for her container and Cole placed it in her hands. She laid it on her stomach and opened it, and the smell of freshly baked bread woke up every one of her sleeping senses.

The sandwich wasn't easy to pick up in this reclined position, but she still managed to take a bite. Her teeth sunk into the soft bread, the smooth avocado, and the tender meat, the tangy aioli bursting with flavor on her tongue. "I think this might be the best thing I've ever eaten."

She took another bite, closing her eyes to devote all her attention to the taste, and she moaned. As soon as she swallowed, she swore she could feel the energy from the sandwich spreading throughout her body. Maybe eventually she would be able to peel herself off this couch again.

Maybe. But first, she'd have to convince her feet to let her stand on them again.

As if Cole could read her thoughts, he scooted forward in his seat, reached out, and started rubbing her feet. She set the sandwich back in its container, dropped her hands to the couch at her sides, and closed her eyes. Cole held her right foot in his strong hands, running them along everywhere that ached, putting just the right amount of pressure in just the right places to make the pain drift away.

As he worked, he said, "Tell me about this presentation that's been running you all ragged."

Brooke couldn't open her mouth to talk. She was in a dream world where Cole's touch worked magic to undo all the stress she'd put on her feet over the past too many days. His touch felt even more incredible now than it ever had before. Delbrina must've figured out that Brooke wasn't going to answer, so she did for her.

"Well, a...company asked a couple of people to come to show them their designs, because they have some space on their racks, and they want to choose someone to fill it."

Good. Delbrina was choosing her words carefully. Brooke relaxed on the couch even more as Cole switched to her left foot, his touch making everything feel right in the world.

"So kind of like a job interview?"

Delbrina said, "Exactly!" at almost the same time Noemi said, "Sure. If you call a singer performing on *The Voice* a 'job interview.'"

Brooke's eyes flew open and she shot Noemi a look. Noemi mouthed *Sorry*, and then took a big bite of her sandwich like she didn't trust herself not to let something slip if her mouth wasn't full.

Delbrina took a sip of her smoothie. "So then Brooke will get all fancied up as Big City Brooke, which she's *very* good at, and then with what we've prepared, she's going to knock the socks off her interviewers. I'm going to tell you right now that after she shows her stuff, the competition is going to be more nervous than a long-tailed cat in a room full of rocking chairs."

"I bet they are," Cole said. "And wow, 'Big City Brooke.' There are not a whole lot of things I'd like more than to see that."

"It's impressive," Noemi said. "I'm a big city girl who hates the snow. Big City Brooke is the reason I was willing to move to Denver, and she's the reason I'm willing to brave these roads an hour in each direction, even in the winter."

"Okay." Brooke laughed nervously and pushed herself to an upright position. For nearly three years, she'd shared with Cole the same side of her that she'd shared with all of Nestled Hollow and that had worked out great. Lately, though, a small part of her wanted to open up more to this man and show him the side of her that no one outside of Noemi and Delbrina had seen. But she just wasn't ready.

"She's a pretty big deal, huh?"

Delbrina waved off his comment like it was nothing. "Noemi's just kissing up to the person who signs her paychecks. You and Brooke have been friends for a long time—I'm sure you've seen the side of her that inspires loyalty well enough."

"That I have."

He gave Brooke a look that melted even the parts of her he hadn't just massaged. His face was full of questions that she knew he didn't want to ask with an audience. She was full of questions too—along with much too big of a desire to finish that kiss— but she wasn't sure if she was ready for the answers.

Cole said he had to head back to the restaurant, so Brooke stood and took a few hobbling steps before her feet decided they were okay enough to stand on them again and walked him to the doorway into the retail shop.

"This was exactly the pick-me-up I needed. Thank you. It was very thoughtful."

He moved his arm forward a few inches like instinct made him want to grab her hand, but he pulled it back. In a quiet voice, he said, "We should probably talk sometime."

Brooke nodded. "We probably should."

As soon as the front door closed behind Cole, Brooke turned around to her offices.

Delbrina, standing beside Brooke, pointed at Noemi. "You, my friend, are going somewhere toasty in a handbasket and you know it."

Noemi folded her arms. "I was just nudging things along. If no one did, ten years from now they still wouldn't be anything more than friends."

"I don't need nudges!" Brooke said. And based on how things were headed under the slide last night, Cole didn't either. Maybe they needed the opposite of nudges.

"Are you ready to start dating him?"

"No. I don't date people from Nestled Hollow."

"Then you need a nudge. Not only did he notice that you needed food, but he brought it for you *and* for the people he knew you cared about. And then the man *rubbed your feet*. I've had plenty of guys rub my back—they do it because they hope they'll get something out of it. But a man who rubs your feet? That he does purely because he cares about you."

Delbrina took a step toward Noemi, turning to face Brooke, and in that one motion went from being on her side to joining Noemi's. "She's got a point. Rubbing your feet? That's nudge-worthy."

Brooke let all of her breath out in a huff and shook her head. She'd come to this battle with no ammo, so fighting was pointless. She walked over to the couch, picked up her phone, and texted Whitney.

> Brooke: Coffee. 2:00. Love a Latte. Please?

Whitney's reply came immediately.

> Whitney: I'll be there with bells on.

She tossed her phone back on the couch. Then she picked up her sandwich because it was a really good sandwich and two bites hadn't been nearly enough.

———

When Brooke got to Love a Latte, Whitney was already there, of course, staying true to her always-early, never-late self, with a hot chocolate with whipped cream on the table in front of her. Tory sat across from Whitney, sipping a mug of something, and a third drink sat on the table.

Brooke slipped into the empty seat and said hi.

Whitney grinned and pushed the third drink toward Brooke. "I told Tory that you've been working non-stop and she said she was going to make you something as strong as you are."

"Please let there also be caramel along with the copious amounts of caffeine."

Whitney laughed and said to Tory, "Looks like you called that one right."

"She always does."

Tory stood up and said, "I'll let you two get to chatting. Enjoy your drinks!"

"No, stay," Brooke said, reaching toward Tory. "Please. I could use your advice, too. There's no one in the shop."

Tory sat back down, seeming as relieved to be off her feet as Brooke was. "What's on your mind?"

"Nothing. Everything." She didn't even know what questions she was wanting answers to. "I've just been working too many hours and being around the same people too much. Everything's confusing, and I needed to get away."

Suddenly she had one question she knew she wanted

to ask Tory. "We're both thirty-two. The same age, yet at very different places in life. Knowing what you know now, if you could go back, would you still choose to have four kids? Even knowing what lay ahead?"

"Why? Are you trying to decide if you want kids?"

Brooke shrugged. "I was raised to not want kids because other things were more important. I'm beginning to think that I might be missing out, though."

Tory thought a moment before answering. "That's a question that no one else can answer for you. But for me — yeah. If I could go back, I'd still do it all over again. Even knowing that my life would get this hard."

Brooke swirled her straw around the whipped cream and caramel, pondering Tory's answer as Whitney and Tory sipped their drinks, giving her time to think.

"It's not just that you're thinking of," Whitney said. "You seem nervous. I've never seen you nervous before. Ever. Spill it."

Brooke let go of her drink and leaned back on her chair. "Dating has never made me nervous. I date people because they're fun and I enjoy their company. It's a social get-together that I have zero expectations for after that moment. If they're available the next time I'm in town, we go on a date. If they're not, we don't. Simple."

"But," Whitney prodded.

"But I'm starting to have feelings for someone and this time it's different. I've never considered dating anyone where there was a potential for a more long-term relationship. I've never dated anyone where there were any stakes at all if it didn't work out, let alone one where they're this high. I don't know what to do."

"So," Tory said, motioning to Whitney, "you decided to seek advice from a woman who, until she met 'the one' was a serial non-dater, and," she motioned to herself, "a single mother of four whose husband left her and hasn't had the time nor the lack of wariness to enter into the dating pool again."

Brooke smiled and sipped her drink, hoping that the caffeine would give her superpowers enough for her day.

Then she noticed the smile spreading across Whitney's face.

Tory said to Whitney, "We're talking about Cole, right?"

Whitney nodded.

"How do you both already know? Did he say something?"

Tory laughed. "No one needed to say anything. He's a good-looking single man, you're a good-looking single woman, you're best friends, and you seem to bring out the best in each other. I think everyone knew that the two of you will eventually figure out that you'd make an amazing couple."

Great. So the town was already rooting for them to get

together and they hadn't even gone on a single date. This was a bad idea.

"And," Whitney added, "I know you well enough to know that Cole is the only person who could possibly make you nervous about dating. And I get it. There is a lot at stake."

"His friendship means a lot to me. I can't risk that."

"Okay," Tory said, "let's say you didn't date for fear of ruining a friendship. Do you think your friendship would continue like it has been for years to come?"

"Of course."

Whitney shook her head. "No. Not with him being as in love with you as he's always been."

"Wait, what?"

"Brooke." Whitney chuckled. "With as good as you are at reading people, you have quite the blind spot when it comes to reading Cole's feelings toward you. And now that you've discovered you have feelings for him, too, you've crossed a point of no return. Your friendship will never be the same."

Brooke's eyes flashed to Tory's to see if it was true. Tory shrugged and nodded.

If that was true, she needed to figure out how she felt about Cole and decide what she was willing to risk and what she was willing to do about it.

eleven

COLE

Cole worked inside the square formed by long banquet tables placed right in the intersection of Center and Main, cooking burgers on one of a half-dozen outdoor grills. He had gotten together with the Keetchs and Joey to plan an easy-to-hold menu for the Take Flight Festival, and they all, including a couple of dozen employees pulled from all three businesses, were preparing meals for the people who would be lining up on both sides of the street any moment now.

When he got the chance to glance up, he looked toward Snowdrift Springs Park—the kites were still in the air, so they had at least a few more minutes. He instructed two of his employees to make sure that the burger and hot dog stations on both sides of the road were ready, two to help with preparing the sub sandwiches, one to check on the vegetable wraps, and a couple to head over to Joey's Pizza and Subs to help haul the first batch of pizzas from his store to the tables.

"They're headed our way," Ed Keetch said, and Cole glanced up just as the last kite he could see in the park nose-dived toward the ground.

A couple of minutes later, all the people who had been at the festivities in the park rounded the corner onto Main Street in a long parade of people holding their kites in the air and shaking them to the beat of the music. As they came down his side of Main Street, he saw Samantha in the parade, dancing with her purple and green kite, her grandma walking alongside her.

She smiled and waved to him as they passed, then called out, "When we come back around, we're going to sit right in front of Best Dressed, okay?"

He gave her two thumbs up and checked on the last of the preparations. After the parade went down Main Street on one side of the creek, then up it on the other side, everyone scattered to find places to sit and watch on the sidewalks in front of the stores and beside the booths. From his station by the food, he searched for Sam in front of *Best Dressed* and found her saying goodbye to her grandma, Brooke at her side. Then the two of them sat down to watch.

The colorful kites for the synchronized kite show rose into the air at First Street, and even Cole and everyone in the food area stopped to watch. The kite fliers made their way down both sides of Main Street, their kites weaving back and forth high in the air, circling into different shapes before scattering and forming something new. He always forgot how impressive the show was every year.

The moment the show finished, the crowds headed to all the activity booths, filling the streets, and the lines at the food area were so long he couldn't see beyond them. Sam and Brooke came through the line, but he barely had a moment to wave hello while trying to keep up with the demand.

When things finally slowed down, he caught a glimpse of Samantha and Brooke playing some kind of game at a booth, and he stopped what he was doing and just watched. The smile that always lit up Sam's face whenever she was around Brooke made his heart happy. And Brooke seemed to genuinely enjoy being around Sam.

Maybe a relationship with Brooke could work. Did he dare try? What if he and Brooke started dating and things didn't work out? Could things just go back to the way they were now?

For a moment as he watched the two of them step up to the next booth, he imagined what life might be like with Brooke. What it would be like to sit down at the dinner table with Brooke and Sam. To curl up on the couch with Brooke in his arms. To share a kiss on that sidewalk every morning before they both parted to go to their own businesses.

"Boss."

He didn't know how it would all turn out. All he knew was that he wanted to try.

"*Boss*," Hani said more insistently, and Cole realized he had been trying to get his attention.

Hani reached behind his back to tie his apron straps. "I'm here to take over. You ready?"

He really was. He gave Hani a few last-minute directions, then made his way out of the food area and jogged down the street to meet up with Sam and Brooke.

"Daddy!" Sam said as he neared. "How do you like my face?"

"It's beautiful. I can't believe you waited in such a long line to have it painted."

She reached out and grabbed hold of Brooke's hand. "Me and Brooke told each other stories to pass the time. I chose to have them paint it like a butterfly because when I was flying my kite, it felt like a butterfly to me. Well, except for all the times I kept crashing it."

Cole met Brooke's eyes and said, "Thank you." The words weren't enough to convey his gratitude for all she did to make Sam's life happier, but he hoped that she understood.

"You're welcome," Brooke said. She seemed to be trying to say more with her words, too, but he couldn't decipher exactly what it was. Then she fumbled in her bag. "I almost forgot—I got a present for you. It finally came today."

She handed him a brown paper gift bag, and he reached inside and pulled out a toy figurine of a dragon wearing a chef's hat. "Oh, wow. I— Brooke, this is quite possibly the coolest thing I've ever owned."

"Let me see, Daddy."

Cole handed the dragon to Sam and she held it cupped in her hands. "He's adorable! Where are you going to put him?"

"Right next to where I work in the kitchen. Thank you, Brooke." Brooke's smile was so beautiful he had a hard time pulling his eyes away from it.

"Grandma says she's coming back to pick me up at eight-thirty," Sam said. "I told her we'd be waiting in front of the restaurant."

Cole glanced at his watch. "It looks like we have time to hit a couple more booths if you'd like."

"Yes!" Sam shouted, jumping a few times, and he suspected that she had won candy at a few of the booths and had already eaten some. "Can Brooke come too?"

Cole looked at his friend. "Do you need to get back to your office?"

She gave him a smile bigger than he'd seen in a couple of weeks. "We made such great progress that we all decided to take the night off."

The three of them walked down Main Street with Sam in the middle, holding both of their hands like they were a family. He shouldn't have been surprised at how right it felt.

They made it to the very last booth before it was time to walk back to the Back Porch Grill. When Susan arrived, Cole hugged Sam, asked her to go to bed as soon as her grandma asked her to, then thanked Susan for taking her to the park earlier and for watching her until he got home tonight.

The responsible part of him, the part that always won out, felt like he should head back to the food area and help clean up. But the part of him that wanted to go to the lantern festival with Brooke was stronger. The night was beautiful, and he wanted nothing more than to be near her. The two of them headed to the food area to check with his employees to make sure they were all good to finish without him.

As they were walking back down Main toward First, Brooke said, "So tell me, Cole Iverson, when you woke up this morning, did your schedule say to help clean up afterward or to delegate?"

He might have blushed a little. "Clean up," he admitted. "Although my employees didn't know that. They were all planning to stay after to get everything put away. Should I have stayed?"

She shook her head. "You shouldn't be at work right

now any more than I should." As they reached First, she looked in the direction the crowds were heading on their trek back to Snowdrift Springs Park for the lantern festival. "I'll race you there."

"After I just showed a remarkable feat of spontaneity by going to this instead of cleaning up?"

"If I had a trophy of someone flinging the ripped-up pieces of a calendar into the air like confetti, I'd award it to you and not make you run. But I've been working too much and not getting enough exercise or fresh air. Race me."

"I've got longer legs, so you won't be able to win."

"I've got..." Brooke seemed to search for anything that might give her the advantage, but couldn't come up with anything. Then her face brightened and she said, "Extra energy fueled by giddiness at finally having a free night. Plus," she held up a finger, "a willingness to cut corners. Go!"

Brooke took off running and Cole chased after her. Instead of heading up the road with the crowds and across to the upper part of the park on lighted streets, she went straight ahead and cut between the Davis's and the Boulters' houses and into an empty field in the dark. As she ran across the open space, he caught up with her and they ran side-by-side. Then she ran down a small incline, jumped over a short stone wall, and through the weeds at the bottom of the park.

After crossing through the middle of Main Street, Snowdrift Springs meandered its way back and forth through Snowdrift Springs Park, and he could see that Brooke was headed straight for it, even though there weren't any pedestrian bridges nearby.

"Risky," he said between panting breaths.

"Feels like a good night for it," Brooke said, followed by a burst of speed.

Cole ran faster too, sprinting to make it to the creek before her. When he got to the edge, he leaped across, landing on the other side. He turned to see Brooke just as she leaped across too, except she didn't land on the other side as solidly as he did and nearly fell backward into the water. He reached out, wrapping his arms around her waist, keeping her from falling.

She breathed fast and heavy from the run, her forearms against his chest, her hands clutching his shirt. "Thanks."

Her closeness felt dangerous to their friendship at the same time it felt so right for the relationship they'd spent three years building. The smell of her perfume and her warm breath against his neck made his skin buzz with energy. He never wanted to let go, but still managed to release her as soon as she got her footing. "These longer legs can't be discounted so easily."

"Maybe," she said. "But neither can this giddiness

that's powering me. It's stronger than one of Tory's quad-shot caramel macchiatos."

"Good, because we're at the wrong side of the park to get a lantern."

As they walked to the upper park and the place where all the people who took the normal path were filing in, Cole asked, "When do you leave for L.A.?"

"In three days. It's not the best timing. There's still so much to do for that presentation I'm giving in New York in a week and a half, but this trip was planned long before I knew they'd ask me to come present."

"Can you cancel this trip or reschedule?"

She shook her head. "If I was just going for the meetings I had set up, then rescheduling might be an option. But I have a friend who is having his first solo fashion show, and I promised I would help."

As they neared the gathering place for the lantern festival, Brooke put a little more space between them, even though the night was getting chilly. Maybe that almost-kiss between the two of them had been a fluke and he'd read it all wrong.

But when they were getting their paper lantern and opening it up, she scooted closer again. The more time they spent together, the more confused he became.

"When you're ready with your lantern," Mayor Stone called out, "gather over here."

Dozens of people gathered on the grass next to

Snowdrift Springs, each pair with a paper lantern. Gloria wove in and out of people, handing out fireplace lighters for everyone to share.

"Paper lanterns have meant a lot of things to a lot of people," the mayor said. "To us here in Nestled Hollow, they've traditionally meant 'When fears are grounded, opportunities take flight.' Our little ones experienced it today with their kites, and now we are with the lanterns. We don't need to hold onto our fears— let them fall to the ground, and we'll spot those opportunities right in front of us." The mayor looked around the group. "Now is everyone ready?"

"Do you want to hold it up and I'll light it?" Brooke asked.

Cole nodded and held it high, and Brooke crouched down under it, lighter poised below the fuel cell.

"Go ahead and light them!"

Brooke looked up at Cole. "Do you have your fears properly grounded?"

He made a show of dropping an invisible something, then stepping on it. She pretended to drop something too, and then ground it into the grass with her shoe. Then she flicked on the lighter and lit the cell before standing up.

They both watched their lantern as the heat from the fire inflated the paper, making the sides expand wider and wider by the moment. The weight in Cole's hand lessened as the lantern swelled until he could feel it pressing against his fingers. Then he let go and they watched as it floated up into the air, glowing in the night sky as it went.

Brooke grabbed his hand and ran, and he followed after. "We have to watch it from a bridge over the water," she said.

When they reached the pedestrian bridge, they stood in the middle, looking up at all the sky lanterns glimmering in the darkness, their lights reflecting in the stream below them.

"It's so beautiful," Brooke breathed.

It was. But not as beautiful as she was. He wished he could tell her that. He had wished for years. But even though he'd made a show of stomping on his fears just barely, he was afraid of starting a conversation about them becoming more than friends, because what if that ended their friendship?

It had been a good two and a half years since realizing he was in love with Brooke. It was tough to keep a secret, but it was worth her friendship. He could do it again. He tucked away the dreams of her one day being a wife to him and a mother to Sam, of kissing her goodbye every morning, of eating dinner together in their home at night, and of falling asleep with her in his arms. He would just brush their almost-kiss off as a fluke, apologize for his part in it, and go back to just being friends.

He turned to face Brooke, leaning against the railing of the pedestrian bridge. "Listen, Brooke," he started, and their eyes met, hers piercing his, the moonlight making her eyes sparkle, the light bathing her cheeks in silver, and she looked so beautiful and perfect, exactly right, that he nearly lost his nerve. He swallowed hard and tried again. "About the other night under the slide, when we almost kissed—"

Brooke stepped right in front of him, her feet in the space between his, and he lost the ability to form words. She reached out and put both hands on the sides of his face, her eyes searching his for something he desperately hoped she was finding.

Then she leaned forward, slowly at first, like she was afraid, then she closed the gap quickly, her lips meeting his with an intensity he hadn't expected. He put his hands around her waist, pulling her closer, his lips matching hers in intensity, pouring all of his hopes into the kiss.

Then her kiss changed to something sweet and tender. Something that years of friendship had cultivated and tended. All of the moments they'd spent together— all the laughing, working, consoling, comforting, listening, playing, and talking— had found their way into this one moment. As her lips moved against his, he knew that whatever fear had sent her rushing into this kiss was gone, replaced with hope, confidence, and a longing that he felt every bit as strongly himself.

She slid her hands down to his neck, and warmth spread throughout his body when her fingertips touched the back of his neck. He could kiss this woman for hours and never let go.

Brooke pulled back from the kiss first, and she let out a happy sigh.

"Wow. This," he whispered, "was not the direction I thought this conversation would go."

BROOKE

Never had Brooke been so nervous to kiss a man before. And never had a man's arms around her waist felt so caring and sweet, strong and protective, essential and right. This man had been such a huge, important part of her life for so long, and now she'd kissed him— for real. From this side of their kiss looking back, it seemed strange that she'd never realized how inevitable it was. How every moment had been leading to this.

Why had she let fear stop her from this for so long?

Like every big risk she'd taken, it left her feeling an intoxicating mix of brave and powerful. But unlike every other risk she'd taken, it felt like the most correct choice she'd made in her life. She sighed and leaned into his side, her head resting on his shoulder, his arms around her.

Cole shifted so she could see his face. "Brooke, this

is...pretty monumental. Are you sure you're okay with this?"

She gave him a smile that she felt with her whole body. "I am."

———

Brooke fell asleep flooded with euphoria and woke that next morning with a start. She hurried to work, managed to get there by seven a.m., and immediately looked up her flight and hotel to see what changes could be made.

Back Porch Grill didn't open until ten, but she knew that Cole showed up to start prepping as soon as he dropped Sam off at school at eight-thirty. She attempted to work on a proposal for her sewing manufacturer, but she found herself mostly pacing and looking at the clock every two minutes.

The moment she knew Cole would be at the restaurant, she walked a block through the back parking lots between Best Dressed in the middle of Main to Back Porch Grill on the corner of First and Main.

Knowing the front door wouldn't be open, she knocked on the back one. When Cole opened it, she said, "I've never been in an exclusive relationship before."

"Good morning, Brooke. Come in." He opened the door wide and held his arm out to his kitchen. How had she never realized before just how good he looked in a button-down and an apron? "I can't say I expected to see you bright and early this morning, knocking on my door to confess your past relationship statuses. But I also know you like spontaneity, so maybe I should've guessed."

"Oh, hi, Lori," Brooke said as she stepped further into the back rooms and realized they weren't alone.

"Don't mind me," Lori said. "I'll just go...fill up the salt shakers in the lobby or something."

As she left the kitchen, Cole reached out and took both of Brooke's hands in his. Now that she was here and talking with him, she inwardly chuckled at the ridiculousness of the urgency she had felt this morning. But still, this was important.

"So," she said, "having never been in a serious relationship before, I'm new at this. Actually, I guess I just assumed, but we never actually talked about it. We're in an exclusive relationship, right?"

Cole smiled like he was trying to keep himself from smiling. "I assumed we were, too. Well, I guess 'hoped' is a better word."

Brooke nodded. So they were on the same page. "Sometime during the middle of the night, my subconscious figured out that in a relationship, it's important to be honest."

"Definitely an important ingredient to a successful relationship."

"So here's the deal. There's more than one side of me.

There's Nestled Hollow Brooke, and there's Big City Brooke. I keep Big City Brooke far away from Nestled Hollow."

Cole nodded. "I've kind of gathered that. But Brooke, we all have different sides to us. Case in point: I've never seen this side of you before, and I had never seen your nervous side before last night." He reached out and ran his knuckles down her cheek.

The touch sent tingles down her spine and she nearly paused just to enjoy it. But no. They had things to discuss. "Right. But those are accidental sides of me. Not a purposefully hidden side of me. The only people here who have seen it are Delbrina and Noemi. Not even Whitney has seen Big City Brooke. But Cole, you've been one of my best friends for nearly three years and now that we're something more, I realized I'm ready for you to see it."

A smile spread across Cole's face that was so big it even made his ears move. "I'm honored. Wow. I would love to see that side of you."

"So come to L.A. with me. You and Sam both. I checked— there are extra seats on my flight, and the hotel has a bigger suite available with a second room."

Cole stood up straighter. "Join you on your trip that's in three days?"

"Two now. I know it's not on your schedule, and this is spontaneity on a bigger scale than I've ever asked of you before."

"You do know I have a restaurant to run. And a daughter in school."

Brooke nodded. "And I know you have capable employees, and it's a short trip. Sam would only miss two days of school. And then you'll see the work side of me like I saw of you when I worked in the restaurant."

Emotions were plainly at war on his face. Fear, probably of leaving his restaurant. Curiosity, probably of seeing this side she'd kept hidden from him. Uncertainty, probably at doing something not on his schedule with such short notice. Care and concern, probably for her. This one was showing even more deeply than his usual, and it made her want to reach out and touch the expression, to experience it with more than just sight.

"I've never been to L.A."

"I used to live there, and I know all the ropes."

"I don't know if it's a trip Sam will enjoy."

"I'll make sure she does."

"I don't know anything about the fashion world."

"A week from now, you'll no longer be able to say that."

Cole paced back and forth in his kitchen, rubbing his chin scruff with his knuckle, probably thinking through the logistics of leaving someone else in charge of Back Porch Grill. "I've always wanted to see Big City Brooke."

"And I've never wanted to show you. Until now."

———

Samantha raced through Best Dressed and into Brooke's offices, wrapping her arms around her in a hug. "I'm so excited that I found out we are going to go on a trip with you *and* I get to try on the dress you made for me. This is the best day ever!"

"I'm just impressed that your dad said yes to going."

Cole chuckled and rubbed the back of his neck. He may have said yes, but he was still unsure. Brooke winked at him.

"Me, too," Sam said. "Good job on talking him into it."

She held out a thumbs-up, so Brooke held out her thumbs-up, and Sam bumped them together.

"You might need help getting the dress on for the first time, so," she grabbed the slip she had lying on the design table and handed it to Sam, "you go put on this, and then I'll come in and help you put the dress over the top of it." She opened the door to the storage room that doubled as a dressing room when needed, then closed it after Sam went in.

As Sam changed, Brooke walked up to Cole and rested her hands on his shoulders, scooting in close. "Hello there."

He wrapped his arms around her. "Us dating is one of the better ideas either of us has had. No Delbrina or Noemi today?"

"They were here earlier. I made them go home at five

because they're loyal to the point that I worried working more hours would kill them both off."

Cole took the rare moment alone and kissed her on the lips, so soft and tender, and Brooke smiled into the kiss.

"I'm ready," Sam called out.

Brooke ran her fingertips from his shoulder down his arm as she walked away from him and went to the back storage room to help Sam.

"Okay," Brooke said, unzipping the dress bag, "are you ready to see it?"

She pulled the dress out and Sam said, "Oh my gosh, oh my gosh, *oh my gosh*! It's just like the dress in the book, only so much better than anyone could have imagined! I can't believe I get to wear this. I can't believe you made this for me. Come on, come on, let's get this on me!"

Brooke laughed and called out in Cole's direction, "I think it's possible she's happy with how it turned out."

She unzipped the dress. "Okay, now when you're putting this on by yourself later, you'll want to hold it up like this, and then gently lower it to the floor. Since it's a fluffy dress, that will help the fluffy parts go outward.

"Now keep holding the shoulder part, and when your arms are straight down, look and see if there's a good enough hole in the middle to step into because you don't want to step on any part of the dress. If there isn't, just put one foot inside, and use it to push the dress out of the way. Yep, just like that.

"Okay, now step inside. Make sure your slip is inside the dress, too, then you can start slowly pulling it up until you can slip your arms inside. Good. And then you might need help pulling the zipper up because it goes pretty high."

"Nope, I'm good at zippers. Watch." Sam pulled the zipper up herself. Brooke smiled, then led her back into the main room.

Brooke enjoyed the look of amazement that crossed Cole's face when he saw his daughter. "Whoa, Sam. Wow."

"I know! Isn't it the most beautiful thing you've ever seen?"

She twirled around once, the dress spinning out around her. Then Brooke led her to the big mirrors.

She had originally chosen a different fabric for the dress. They'd even cut it out and started sewing the bodice, but then she found a fabric that she knew would be even more incredible. Noemi and Delbrina had gotten used to her last-minute changes over the years, but they both showed some frustration at the change when they had so little time to work with.

But as much work as the change in fabric was, it had been the right choice. It was perfect for the dress—a shimmering, iridescent, sheer material with purple undertones over a deep purple bodice and skirt, with layers and layers of sheer fabric.

She had sewn crystal beads in the shape of leaves up the bodice like vines up a castle wall, and fabric flowers blossomed out from the waist, cascading down the skirts.

"I can't believe I'm wearing this," Sam said. "I would cry happy tears, but I don't want them to get on this dress. It's just too pretty."

"You can keep looking in the mirror— I just need to mark some adjustments while you're looking, okay?"

Sam nodded and Brooke got to work. A few of the flowers didn't sit in just the right place, so she pinned to mark each spot, and she checked to make sure all the layers of the skirt were sitting correctly and that they ended at the same hemline.

"How did you know what size I was?"

"Well," Brooke said as she worked, "my mom started a company that makes cosmetics, or makeup. Do you know the Van Zandt Department Store?"

"Yep! My dad took me once when we went to Denver."

"When I was about your age, they let her do a pilot program in one of their stores, to see how people liked her stuff. So about twice a week for a year, she went to that store to show customers her products, and then started a new program where they do makeovers for people. She always went on Saturdays and took me.

"I wasn't interested in cosmetics, but this was at their

biggest store in New York City, and so they had a design department, where people could come in and have dresses custom-made for them. I always hung out with the woman who did that while my mom was busy. She would take her client's measurements, and then she had a dress form that she would adjust to those exact measurements.

"When she didn't have customers, she let me choose a customer who was shopping and try to adjust the form to match the person without being able to measure them first, and I got really good at it."

"I want to get really good at something like that." She paused for a moment as Brooke worked on her dress, then said, "My dad told me that you and him are dating right now."

Brooke glanced at Cole and he hid a smile.

"And what do you think about that?"

"Well, he told me that you might be hanging out together more often, which, by the way, I'm totally cool with. And he said that you two would probably have hugs and kisses. Oh! That reminds me, Daddy, I forgot to tell you that I already came up with the *Sam's Special* for tomorrow."

"Oh yeah?"

She nodded. "You know those chicken salad sandwiches that you serve at lunch sometimes? It's like that, only you take the chicken part and roll it up inside the croissant while it's still dough, and then you cook the chicken inside it. I don't know— you might have to change the stuff you put in it. So I was thinking about what it would be called, and since croissants always look like a smiling mouth to me, we can either call it 'Smoochie Surprise,' or 'Kissing Croissants.'"

"Sam!" Brooke said, a little alarmed at the thought of people knowing they were dating.

Sam turned both of her hands up in a shrug. "What? It sounds to me like a good way to celebrate that you two are dating. And that way, other people in town can join in on the celebrating."

Cole's booming laughter bounced off the walls as Brooke's cheeks burned.

"So," Sam said, "what will we be doing on this trip?"

Brooke put in a few pins, adjusting the hemline on one side. "It's a short trip and I already have a lot packed into it. We can't make it any longer because you need to get back to school, your dad needs to get back to the restaurant, and I need to get back to preparing for my presentation in New York. So you'll mostly be with me as I do my normal stuff. I've got to talk to a couple of boutiques, have lunch with my dad because he lives there, and one night we get to dress up fancy and go to a fashion show on the runway."

Cole raised an eyebrow. "So the rumors of you only going out of town to go to parties is false?"

"Not false," Brooke asserted, pointing a pin in his

direction. "I *do* go to parties when I'm out of town. I like parties. It's where designers get together to network."

"Can I wear this when we dress up fancy?"

"Of course. Okay, now go get changed, and watch out for any pins."

As Sam went back to change, Brooke stood up and went to Cole, surprised by the look on his face. "Oh! You're nervous. About the trip. Why?"

"It's a lot of things not really in my comfort zone. I don't even own any fancy clothes."

Brooke smiled. "Don't worry— I've got everything you need."

thirteen

COLE

Cole had never flown first class before. It was actually kind of cool, and completely unexpected. It hadn't even occurred to him that it might be normal for Brooke.

He'd also never been driven to his hotel by one of those drivers holding up a sign in baggage claim with someone's name on it. That was when this trip started to feel a little unreal. But Brooke said that driving in Los Angeles was insane, and after experiencing it, he could see why she chose not to drive there when she didn't have to.

But it was walking into the hotel that really started to make him uncomfortable. The lobby looked expensive and his restaurant and the next two shops could probably all fit inside.

As they walked up to their rooms with the bellhop,

which he had thought only happened in movies, Brooke said, "I had a one-bedroom reserved, and on such short notice, I could only up it to a two-bedroom. So you won't be able to have your own room, Sam, but I did have them bring you a cot, so at least you'll have your own bed."

Cole had pictured a cramped hotel room, complete with a busy patterned bedspread, a desk, and a door that locked on both sides and opened into the other hotel room, a cot squished in between the bed and the wall.

But the bellhop opened double doors into a giant living area where everything was bright and open, and windows ran floor to ceiling along the far wall, showing an impressive view of the night lights of the city. A doorway on the left led to one bedroom, and a doorway on the right led to another.

Brooke thanked the bellhop, tipped him, and told him they had ordered food in the car and to send it up when it arrived, all while Sam raced through the hotel rooms, exploring.

The food that arrived was pretty good. He wasn't used to eating food that someone else had cooked, but he had to admit that after an exhausting evening of traveling after a long day at work, it was nice to have food cooked and brought right to him.

When they finished eating, Brooke stretched. "We've got a busy day tomorrow, and we'll need to be ready to walk out the door by eight-thirty. We should probably get to bed soon."

"Why don't you run and get your pajamas on, Samster? I'll be in to read to you in just a minute."

Sam hugged Brooke, thanked her again for the awesome plane ride and riding in the fancy car, and staying in the fancy hotel. Then she skipped off to their room.

Before the food had come, Brooke had changed into yoga pants and pulled her hair up into a chaotic bun. He'd seen the look several times when they'd gotten together at one or the other's house to watch movies over the years.

But still, as he looked at her on the oversized couch, tired from a long string of working too many hours, he couldn't imagine anyone more beautiful.

He reached out a hand and pulled her to her feet, then wrapped his arms around her.

"I'm glad you came," she said.

"I'm glad you used all your powers of persuasion to get me to come."

"Not *all*—I have a pretty extensive array of powers of persuasion. You haven't even seen half of them yet."

He laughed. "Then I hope you never turn to a life of crime and want me to be your accomplice, Brooke McClellan."

Brooke glanced at his lips, and he thought of how many times he'd hoped that one day he would be able to kiss Brooke goodnight. He felt a little out of place in such an extravagant setting, but he'd take it. He put a knuckle under her chin and leaned down and kissed her. "Goodnight, Brooke."

"Goodnight, Cole."

———

They spent the morning traveling to different boutiques throughout L.A., and Cole found out that a boutique was actually just a smaller clothing store. He didn't know why they didn't just call them dress shops— it made so much more sense.

At each place, Brooke charmed the owners, who all seemed to have heard of her already, and left a book behind showing her designs, all while he and Sam wandered around the store, Sam *ooh*ing and *ahh*ing at all the dresses.

"Oh," Brooke said as they left the last shop, looking down at her phone. "My dad said he had a meeting pop up that he hadn't planned on, and wants to know if we can have lunch in his office instead of at the restaurant. Is that okay?"

"Sure." Cole had met Brooke's dad a few times before —he came to visit Brooke every six months or so, and they always came into the restaurant to eat. He usually showed up in jeans and a button-down, but the guy had perfected the power pose, so meeting him in a more casual location than a fancy restaurant where he'd already be feeling out of place sounded better anyway.

At least it had until their driver pulled up to Brooke's dad's offices. Cole angled his head so he could see the name on the side of the tall building, and a lump formed in his throat. "*McClellan Properties?*" His head whipped in her direction. "Your dad, Ben, is *Benton* McClellan?"

Brooke cringed.

"Brooke, your dad is *the* Benton McClellan and you never told me?"

"He's just my dad. You've met him before— it's not a big deal."

She opened the door and the three of them got out. Cole took a deep breath, squared his shoulders, and walked with them inside the building. The receptionist recognized Brooke immediately and called up to her father's office to let him know they were there, and then they took the elevator up to his floor.

This was not the hallway lined with office doors that he had been imagining. This was a modern, beautiful, open space with conversation areas, conference rooms with glass walls, and a view that rivaled their hotel's.

Brooke's dad came out to meet them and he and Brooke hugged. If Cole thought he was intimidating in jeans and a button-down, he should've guessed how much more intimidating he'd be in a suit and a power tie. This *was* a big deal. And right now, he knew he really didn't belong in this world.

"You remember my friend Cole from Back Porch Grill?"

Cole reached out and shook Mr. McClellan's hand. "Nice to see you again."

"And this is his daughter, Samantha."

Samantha shook his hand, too, and then said, "I like your building. It's super pretty. Especially that plant over there."

Benton McClellan turned to glance at the plant and then said, "Why thank you. I'm charmed to meet you."

Brooke's dad led them into one of the conference rooms, where a buffet along one wall was loaded with food. He handed them each a plate, then started loading up his own, so they each followed suit and then sat down at the conference table.

"I'm guessing you've been pretty busy preparing for your Van Zandt presentation. Congratulations again on making the top five. I'm super proud of you."

The shock hit Cole. Her presentation was to Van Zandt? He might not know a lot about the fashion world, but he knew enough to know that having Van Zandt consider carrying your clothing line was huge. No wonder she had been working so many hours. He was feeling more and more out of her league by the moment. He looked down at the sweet and sour pork and spring rolls on his plate and didn't think he'd be able to take a single bite.

"Thanks, Dad. We're pretty excited about it."

"How's business? Have you gotten any business offers lately?"

"It's good, and just one."

"Are they bigger or smaller than you?"

"Same size."

"You're not accepting the offer, right?"

"I've already told him no."

"That's my girl."

"You don't usually bring people from home when you visit." He pointed his chopsticks between Brooke and Cole and Samantha. "Tell me the story."

Brooke reached out and put her hand in Cole's. "Cole and I recently started dating, and I wanted to introduce him to this side of things a bit."

"Then I'm very glad to meet you officially. How long have you two been dating?"

The question was directed at Cole, so he answered, "Um, four days."

Mr. McClellan raised both eyebrows and turned to Brooke. "Four days. So I guess you're moving pretty fast then if you're already taking him with you on a business trip."

Brooke squeezed Cole's hand and chuckled. "Dad,

we've been best friends for nearly three years. If anything, I'd say we're moving pretty slow."

"So." Mr. McClellan took a bite of his General Tso's chicken. "Tell me why you're good enough to date my daughter."

Cole had been asking himself the same question since boarding the plane last night, so his answer came quickly. "I'm fairly certain I am not." He probably should've sold himself to Benton McClellan, and Brooke's dad would probably think he was taking the easy way out by not, but right then, Cole couldn't think of a single reason he could tell him.

Brooke's dad let out a booming laugh. He clapped Cole on the back and said, "I'm glad you understand that right from the start."

———

Back at the hotel, Brooke handed both him and Samantha a garment bag and told them to go get ready. The suit in his was very nice. And, as he knew to expect, fit him perfectly.

He may not belong in this world, but he was sure looking good in it this afternoon. *Really* good. He kept turning from side to side in his full-length mirror and wondered where he could get away with wearing a suit like this. He'd be willing to wear it pretty much anywhere. Like to work. Or grocery shopping. Or to take his turn being the crossing guard at Nestled Hollow Elementary.

"We're almost ready," Brooke called out from her room where she was helping Sam with her hair.

Cole walked into the living area from his room and leaned against the doorway like he was a celebrity on a magazine cover, ready to blow Brooke away with how great he looked.

And then she walked out of her room, and his shoulder slipped off the doorframe and he had to catch himself before falling face-first into it. "Wow. You...wow. Brooke. You look incredible."

Her dress was a deep green and shimmered in the light. The top only went over one shoulder, leaving the other bare, and the rest was form-fitted down to her hips before it went more wavy, shorter on one side and nearly to her ankle on the other. She looked elegant. Like royalty.

"I would like to present...Princess Samantha!"

Samantha strutted out of the room just then, wearing the dress that Brooke had made, her hair up on top with lots of curls all around. She struck a pose with her hand on her hip and a smile spread across her face. "Aren't I beautiful?"

"As the stars in heaven," Cole said.

"And look at Brooke—she's as beautiful as I am!"

"That she is."

When they arrived at the building for the fashion

show, Cole and Brooke walked arm-in-arm, Sam holding his other hand, and he felt much more confident than he had when walking into Brooke's father's offices. Maybe he should've gone to meet him wearing this suit.

But the confidence that came with the suit waned a bit when they entered the chaos that apparently exploded backstage at a fashion show an hour before people would begin to arrive. Cole clutched Sam's hand as models—mostly men— hair and make-up artists, and assistants hurried everywhere they went, shouting instructions and bringing up issues, and using lingo he had never heard before.

"Brooke," a tall, thin, impeccably-dressed man said as he hurried to them. He hugged her, and said, "How was your flight? Please tell me fabulous. And did you think any more about joining forces with me? All these men in finely tailored suits sure would look good walking on stage with a woman in a finely tailored dress next to them."

"Your suits are so well designed that they don't need anything else to look good. Ian Bancroft, I would like you to meet Cole Iverson and his daughter, Samantha. Cole and I have recently started dating."

The two men shook hands and Ian looked at Brooke. "*Dating*, as in exclusive?"

She nodded, and Ian took a better look at Cole. "Well, it's a pleasure to meet the man who managed to get Brooke McClellan to agree to a partnership." Ian turned to Sam and put both hands over his mouth as he gasped. "My goodness, this might be the most radiant girl I've ever seen. Brooke, did you design this dress?" When Brooke nodded, he said, "How do you feel about a pre-show walk down the runway to get people excited about seeing some fancy clothes?"

"Are you serious?" Sam asked. "I can go out there and let everyone see me in my beautiful dress? For reals?"

Ian looked to both Cole and Brooke for confirmation, then to Sam. "For real."

For the next hour, Cole stood by himself, feeling awkward and out-of-place, as one of the assistants taught Sam how to walk the runway and Brooke went from person to person who were each having problem after problem, fixing things and leaving a calm easiness in her wake.

She was so at home here, was so good at what she did, and was so adored by everyone around her that he could see why this was such a powerful draw to her. No wonder she went out of town so often. She got love and adoration on a grand scale here.

It wasn't simply that Brooke was out of his league. It was that he had grown up in a world where the sport she played didn't even exist. Even offering her all he had, he couldn't give her what this world was giving her. He couldn't compete with this.

BROOKE

The thrill, the excitement, and the energy of the show coursed through Brooke. For as much as she had been dreading that this trip was going to take away from her prep time for the Van Zandt presentation, she realized it was exactly what she needed to refuel herself.

As the crowds entered the building and mingled in the ballroom as they found their seats, Brooke sought out Cole, who was leaning against a wall, watching all the action going on backstage. In a room filled with male models in suits— men whose actual job description was to look incredible in a suit— Cole still stood out as the most attractive. His suit perfectly accented his broad shoulders and a physique made strong by his days spent in near-constant movement.

But the kindness in his eyes and the genuine concern

he had for people that seemed to emanate from him set him apart from everyone else. His actions and his generosity in not only the way he treated others but in the way he saw others showed through every feature and had truly made his face the most beautiful she had ever seen.

She grabbed his lapels and grinned as she moved in close. "You, sir, are looking mighty fine. How would you feel about walking down the runway? That suit you're wearing is one Ian designed."

The look of alarm that crossed Cole's face made her joking question completely worth it. "Raine did a great job teaching Sam how to pose. I bet she would come to teach you, too."

Cole laughed nervously, his eyes darting around the room. "Uh...I don't think that's such a great idea."

"You're right." She sighed and glanced at the men in suits, then let her eyes fall on the beautiful man in front of her. "You probably shouldn't. Then everyone wouldn't be able to take their eyes off you, and that wouldn't be fair to the men who came here to model."

She smiled when she saw the smile it put on his face. He seemed less overwhelmed by the goings-on backstage, especially since things quieted down when guests started arriving. "Are you game for doing some mingling with the press before we find our seats?"

They checked on Sam, who seemed thrilled to be backstage and not at all nervous about the runway. They let her know that they would be watching from the audience and headed out to meet and greet.

Brooke always liked to socialize with the press, buyers, and others in the fashion world who attended. These were people who chose to promote fashion, and she was grateful for every one of them. She had met many of the people who were in attendance at other events, and it was fun to see them again. As they went from person to person, though, she noticed that Cole wasn't saying much, and she could tell that he was feeling out of place.

Ian's announcer, Silas, stepped up to the microphone at the side of the stage and everyone took that as their cue to find their seats. Once Brooke had let Ian know she was bringing two guests, he had provided her with a couple of prime seats right at the end of the runway.

Once Cole and Brooke and everyone else were seated and quieted, Silas said, "As a pre-show bonus to get you in the mood to see some incredible suits, I am pleased to announce that we've got a special guest to warm you up. I would like to introduce nine-year-old Samantha, wearing a one-of-a-kind, By the Brooke original."

Sam stepped onto the runway just then and Cole grabbed Brooke's hand. He didn't need to be nervous for her, though, because Sam strutted onto the raised platform, looking every bit as confident as seasoned veterans, and showing way more personality than any of them ever did. She reached the end of the runway, put one hand on a cocked hip and the fingertips on her other hand by her ear, elbows out, looking up in the air.

The crowd responded with cheers— something she rarely saw when a model came out—and everyone took pictures. Then Sam held out two thumbs-up, blew the crowd a kiss, then turned and strode back to the other end of the runway and off the stage.

The crowd ate it up. She'd never seen a group so primed to see the designs about to take the stage as this group was. Brooke turned and smiled at Cole. "You've managed to raise an incredibly confident little girl at a time when that isn't always so easy."

He looked deeply into her eyes, searching, and then said, "Thank you for giving her this. She's going to remember it forever."

"It was definitely my pleasure. I'll go get her so you can tell her how great she did and the two of you can watch the show together while I help backstage."

By the time the show had finished, Brooke was still buzzing with energy. Ian had called her on stage at the end, and she smiled extra big when she saw Cole beaming at her and Sam waving wildly.

When the show ended and all the models made it backstage again, Ian turned to her. "You're coming to the after-party, right?"

"Not this time. I think we've probably worn Sam

completely out, especially since we came from a different time zone."

Ian pouted. "But that's when I was planning to talk you into being my business partner."

Brooke laughed and put an arm on his shoulder. "Ian, even if you tried the whole time, tonight's party wouldn't be enough to talk me into a merger. Lone wolf, remember?"

"I'm not giving up." He nodded in the direction of the guests in the ballroom. "You may be a lone wolf, but you also said you'd never date anyone exclusively. Things change."

Brooke glanced in that direction as well, even though they couldn't see into the ballroom.

"How's it going with your man?"

Brooke sighed. "Good. But we haven't been dating long, and I think this trip might've been too soon. I want him to know what he's getting into, but I don't know. I get the sense that he's not liking what he's seeing. They say that opposites attract, and that's probably what made us become friends. But maybe we're *too* different for a relationship to work."

"I hope not. Because you two are as beautiful together as silk and a man's tie."

———

Sam had been so exhausted that she'd fallen asleep while Cole had been reading to her. He crept out of the room and shut the door quietly.

"There's an old zombie movie on that we haven't seen before," Brooke said from where she'd curled up on the couch, remote in hand. "Want to play 'What happens next?' The hotel left a basket of snacks, including microwave popcorn," she held up the bowl, "which I've already made. I figured when we pause for the first 'What happens next,' whoever is wrong has to eat popcorn until round two using these." She picked up the chopsticks from their dinner the night before. "And then in round two, whoever is wrong has to dip their popcorn in this concoction I made out of coffee creamer, sugar, and soy sauce."

An amused smile was playing on Cole's face as he listened, then he nodded. "Okay, but only if, for round three, whoever is wrong has to eat popcorn while dancing, Pulp Fiction-style."

They sat down to watch the movie like they had dozens of times in the past, but this time, she nestled into Cole's side and laid her head on his shoulder.

She knew that she was risking all of the fun traditions of their friendship by dating him when things could potentially go very wrong. But right now, she didn't care. Right now, all she could think about was how much she enjoyed snuggling into him, and how she wasn't the least bit sad that she hadn't gone to the after-party.

———

After taking Cole and Sam along to two more meetings with boutique owners the next morning, they got back in the car and she handed the driver a paper with the address to the refugee center she'd first visited a few years ago.

"One last stop," Brooke said, "then we'll get some lunch before heading to the airport."

When they pulled up to the building and got out of the car, Sam looked at the sign on the building and cocked her head to the side. "What's a *refugee?*"

"It's someone who had to leave their country," Cole said, "usually because of war or something else that has made it where it's not safe to live there anymore."

Brooke nodded. "Many of the people who come here as refugees don't have anything and often don't even speak English. This is a place I found where people can come and get help."

"And today we're going to help them?" Sam asked.

"We are." Brooke pushed the door open. "Sometimes when I come here, I'll help teach English. Other times, I'll help people find clothing to wear to a job interview, help them to fill out some forms, or help match them up with some services they need. It's a surprise every time."

They checked in with Sema, a woman who was frequently there when Brooke came and was currently helping a man fill out a form. "Brooke, I'm so glad you stopped in today. All my volunteers are busy, and there's a couple over there who could use some help." Sema nodded to the computer area, where a husband and wife were trying to work on something with three little kids climbing on them and trying to push buttons. "Before having to flee their home, they ran a restaurant together. They're trying to write a resume to get a job here."

Cole immediately perked up. "I'll help them."

Brooke smiled. "Sam and I will keep the kids entertained while you do."

She and Sam went behind the counter where she knew they kept the toys and pulled out some building blocks, toy cars, and Little People. They set up the toys on the floor in view of the computers so the kids had no problem running to them to play. They helped the three little kids — girls who looked like they were five or six and a boy who was about three— build practically an entire city for the people to live in and the cars to drive around in.

"This reminds me of the shelter in Mountain Springs," Sam said.

Brooke looked at Sam as she walked one of the Little People next to the person one of the little girls was walking. "The homeless shelter?"

Sam nodded. "My dad makes food for them a lot, and

he takes me with him every couple of weeks. We dish up the food and sometimes there are little kids there, too, so I play with them."

Brooke looked over at Cole as he pointed at something on the screen, a smile on his face as he helped the people. "Your dad's a pretty cool guy."

The two hours they had to spend passed too quickly, and Brooke was happy to see that it seemed to be that way for Cole and Sam, too. As they walked out of the building, Cole put his hand in hers. "Do you always come here?"

"Whenever I'm in Los Angeles. In every city I visit, I search for a place to donate money. It's not always a refugee center— I just find a place that speaks to my heart. Then no matter how packed the trip is, I find at least two hours to spend volunteering there. It keeps me remembering what is truly important, instead of thinking that fashion is. Fashion and fancy dresses aren't what make the world go around. People are."

Cole gave her a look that, for the first time since they'd met, she couldn't quite read. The look seemed...conflicted. And then the look was gone and he smiled and squeezed her hand.

COLE

ole had just finished chatting with Sam about school, got her started on her homework at the bar, and headed back into the kitchen when he heard a text come in on his phone. He pulled out his phone and smiled when he saw it was from Brooke.

> Brooke: I have some time right now. Can we get together with Sam to plan activities for her party?

Cole sighed. Brooke knew he was at work right now. And she knew that his schedule was tight enough that he couldn't just make a last-minute change like that. He sent a reply back to her.

> Cole: I'm doing dinner prep. 7:00 work instead?

> Brooke: No. :(

> Brooke: I have to be back in the office at
> 6:30 for a video conference.

He hated spur-of-the-moment changes in plans and how they wreaked havoc on everything. He thought through all he and Hani had to do to get the kitchen ready for the dinner rush before Heather arrived at five-thirty to take his place, and it was too much. Especially because it had been a rough, stressful day after getting behind so much from an unplanned trip to Los Angeles. He had been on edge all day.

But they needed to get this party planned, and he wasn't sure when Brooke would be available again. After he'd read to Sam last night, he'd spent the rest of the night looking up party ideas and couldn't wait to share them with Sam and Brooke. He sent a text to Heather asking if she could come in at five instead. Thankfully, he got a quick "Sure thing," back from her.

> Cole: Okay, I think I have everything
> worked out so I can be off at 5:00. Will
> that work?

Brooke responded with two thumbs-up emojis, so Cole texted his mother-in-law to let her know that she didn't need to stop by the restaurant to pick up Sam and then started prepping the food double-time so he could finish early.

He kept looking out to the lobby to check on Sam and fifteen minutes later, he saw Brooke come in and sit next to her. He glanced at the clock— it was barely after four. He was surprised that Brooke had the extra time to hang out with Sam before they were meeting.

Since he knew Sam was being taken care of in the lobby, Cole threw all his attention into prepping quickly, so as soon as Heather showed up, he was ready to leave. When he left the kitchen, he took a table and chairs in the side room where the tower slide was, so they could plan in the room where it would happen.

"Daddy," Sam said, "you are going to be so excited. Me and Brooke talked about the party and we practically have the whole thing planned now."

Cole's eyebrows drew together. "You already planned it?" He tried to not let the hurt and disappointment come out in his voice. He told Brooke he couldn't get free until five. Why did they start early?

"Yep! We decided to just have a bunch of fun things, and kids can go to whatever they want to go to. We can set up musical thrones, pin the kiss on the frog, a dress-up relay race, and a game where we blow up a bunch of balloons and put toy dragons inside. And we get those plastic swords that are like this long and give one to everyone, and then you have to try to free the dragons by stabbing the balloon to pop it and set the dragon free."

Instead of the fun party he'd been imagining all along, this was sounding like it was going to be pure chaos.

"Sam," Brooke said, her eyes on Cole, "I think your dad has some ideas for the party he'd like to share."

"You do?" Sam said, scooting her chair in and putting her hands on the table, all attention on him. "Tell us!"

He shot Brooke a grateful look, happy that she always picked up on things like that. "I was looking on the internet last night and I found a bunch of ideas. This is a big space. I thought we could have a bunch of different stations all around the room. I can make some giant sugar cookies in the shape of crowns, or dukes and duchesses, or those staffs that royalty holds, or even a glass slipper. Then one of the stations can be decorating the cookies.

"At another station, we could have it be about Rapunzel's long hair, and cut three really long pieces of yarn and tie a knot at one end. Then we could split everyone up in fours, and one person would hold the end with the knot, and the other three would each hold one of the other ends, and then the three people would have to weave in and out of each other to braid the long hair.

"Oh, you know those paper crowns that you can size to fit your head? Well, I found some gems with sticky backs. We could have a crown decorating station where everyone gets to design their own.

"And then, I don't know, a coloring station or something. And, of course, a station where they go down the tower slide."

Sam was grinning. "Those are great ideas, too!"

He was pretty darn proud of himself for coming up with such a great list of ideas for a ten-year-old girl's party. He'd had his eyes on Sam while he'd been explaining them, but now that he glanced at Brooke, he noticed that she had shifted back in her chair. He scratched his temple. "You don't like them?"

"No," Brooke said, sitting up straighter. "I think they're great ideas. It's just that twenty-one kids are coming to this party, and I bet they're going to be bouncing off the walls. I think you might want to channel that energy into playing more active games. If you try to get them to do a bunch of activities where they have to sit and calmly work on crafts, it might backfire."

Cole shook his head. He might have thought that at some point, too. "I've helped out at Sam's school parties before. They always do stations so that the kids don't get too wild and crazy."

"But that's at *school*. A place where they are used to having to sit and calmly work on things. You get them in a different environment, and sugar cookie decorating is going to turn into an activity of throwing the candies around the room or seeing who can get the most frosting on each other. If you have lots of high-energy games spread all around, not only will they have more fun, but they won't be spending their energy in ways that are even crazier."

Cole shook his head. Brooke seemed to be getting frustrated, but he'd experienced enough parties to know he was right. "If you take twenty-one already excited kids and have them do something wild, you'll unleash chaos."

He could tell she had more to say, but instead, she just gave him a nod. "I'm sure you're right." Her phone buzzed and she picked it up off the table, glanced at it for a moment, then said, "I know I was supposed to leave for New York in four days. But I'm sorry; it looks like I'll be leaving tomorrow morning instead. And I can't stay any longer tonight."

Brooke pushed back her chair and stood up, then leaned over and hugged Sam. "I'm so sorry I have to go. I'll see you in six days." She held a hand out toward Cole for a moment, but before he even had a chance to stand up or reach out his hand to hold hers, she'd dropped it, turned, and walked out of the room and out of the restaurant.

An uncomfortable heat burned in Cole's chest as he stood and watched Brooke walk out, and it was soon joined by a heaviness in his stomach and a feeling of utter wrongness. He could tell that there was so much more to Brooke's leaving than a simple disagreement. But it was still very much about him.

Cole hadn't noticed that Sam had stood up until she wrapped both her arms around his arm and leaned her head against it. He looked down to see a tear rolling down her cheek. "Sam," he said, knowing how much this must be affecting her. "Are you okay?"

"She said she was going to ask you about having me go to her house tomorrow night to work on decorations." Her voice was quavering, about to break. "She said we were, and now we aren't. My fairy godmother isn't going to be around to get ready for the party, just like in the book." Sam let go of his arm and turned and buried her face in his side.

Cole put his hand on her back to comfort her as she shook with silent sobs. Sam was always sad when Brooke left on trips. But after all the extra time they had been spending together because of the party and the trip and the fact that he and Brooke were dating now, this was different.

And this time, she had made plans with Sam and then walked away from them. This time was hurting her so much more.

But it wasn't just the way that Sam felt that was causing his heart to hurt. It was also the look on Brooke's face right before she got that text. It was fear, and it scared him.

He could tell by the shallowness of Sam's hitched breathing that she was trying hard not to cry. Knowing

Sam, she was probably thinking of his feelings and how this probably hurt him, too, so she wasn't wanting to cause him more pain by showing that she was upset. Which only served to make him feel worse. He held his arm around her a little bit tighter, hoping that comforting Sam would also help his own heart.

sixteen

BROOKE

A s Brooke left the side room of Back Porch Grill in her attempt to leave, she ran into the socializing crowd of people waiting to be seated in the restaurant. She saw an opening and maneuvered around a couple of people to get there, but then two people who didn't notice her intense need to leave but did notice each other came together to hug, cutting her off. She went around them, only to get stopped by Mrs. Davenport's hand on her arm.

"So good to see you, Brooke, honey! I heard you and Cole were dating and I just wanted to let you know that I think that is wonderful, just wonderful."

Hannah, a woman in her mid-twenties who had her hand slipped into her husband's, piped in and said, "We agree. Tyler and I have been rooting for you two for a long time."

From the other side of the waiting area, Clifton, a big man with a booming voice, said, "When I saw the two of you back there cooking together the other day, even *my* heart melted a little bit."

Brooke smiled and nodded and said thanks and tried to be gracious all while trying her hardest to get out of the building as quickly as possible and away from the frustrating partnership and the people who wouldn't stop talking about it.

Finally, she made it to the door and burst out onto the cool evening air of Main Street.

Her whole life, her dad had told her that equal partnerships didn't work out. And, even though it had been a small disagreement and not something even remotely life-altering, it still showcased that fact. Disagreements were bound to happen. And as equals in a relationship, there wasn't one with authority. Seniority. Veto power.

This was one small issue, but in a long-term relationship, they were bound to run into dozens more, and with much bigger consequences.

The text message she had gotten had been from Delbrina and just said that they had news to tell her and to come back soon. But after her mental image of a lifetime spent with Cole, where any decision they would face moved at the speed of a committee, the text from

Delbrina had provided a good opportunity to leave. She just needed to get away and refocus.

As Brooke walked through Best Dressed and back into her offices, Noemi and Delbrina raced up to her, practically bouncing on their feet, eyes sparkling.

"We just got some great news," Delbrina said.

Noemi nodded "Really great news. Remember how you said that Van Zandt probably asked for so much to be done and gave an incredibly tight timeline because it would tax each business enough that they would find any flaws? Well, it worked. Lake and Lane just dropped out."

Brooke blinked, stunned by the unexpected news. Then she looked back at Noemi and Delbrina. "Lane and Lake? Really? That brand is amazing. I thought they had a good chance to win. They dropped out? Did you hear why?"

"I'm friends with Lane's assistant," Delbrina said, her words coming out in an excited rush. "And she told me that it's been a month of Sundays since Lane and Lake agreed on anything. Lake thinks there's a tree stump in a Louisiana swamp with more business sense than Lane. And Lane thinks Lake is as proud as a peacock and about as useful as a screen door on a submarine. So they each pitched a hissy fit with a tail on it, and now they're calling it quits."

"They're going to dissolve the entire company?" Brooke asked.

"They're fixin' to."

Brooke's legs couldn't hold her up any longer so she collapsed into one of the padded chairs.

"This is great news," Noemi said. "Why don't you look happy?"

No. This was *not* great news. Brooke had no problem at all competing against anyone in a fair competition. Having competition drop out didn't excite her. Instead, having a fellow company fail made her business heart hurt. And seeing an amazing partnership of two brilliant minds fall apart because they couldn't agree caused a pang of fear to pierce her.

seventeen

COLE

Sam's natural state was one of happiness. So Cole knew that no matter what happened that made her feel a different emotion, it wouldn't be long before she would be back to being happy. She had never been a child to mope, wallow, or pout.

So it alarmed him when Sam woke up the next morning and was still so sad. He did everything he could think of that usually made her laugh, including making her smiley pancakes, using crazy voices to pretend like the pancakes were telling her jokes, and even flipping the pancakes high in the air as he turned them over. But nothing worked. Sure, she gave him some attempts at smiles to acknowledge his efforts, but nothing made her smile a genuine smile.

They finished getting ready for school and work, and

he drove Sam to Nestled Hollow Elementary. When he pulled into a spot at the drop-off zone in front of the school, Sam reached a hand between the two seats and said, "Hand hug," like she always did. He reached over and gave her hand a goodbye squeeze.

He was about to pull away, but movement caught his eye and he looked over at Sam, who was waving for him to wait. And then, even though she knew it was against the safety rules, she came around to the driver's side of the car and opened his door. Without a word, she leaned in and gave him a tight hug, holding on longer than he expected.

As he hugged her back, he said, "I'm sorry things are tough right now."

She released the hug, then gave him a sad smile and said, "I'm sorry they are for you, too, Daddy." Then she hurried into school.

He shut the door and had almost pulled out of the school lot before the hurt and loneliness hit him hard. Being focused on Sam and her emotions had allowed him to ignore his own, and now that she was off to school, he was feeling it. Brooke might not have even left for the airport yet, but he was still feeling the pain of her leaving so much more strongly than he ever had during their years of friendship.

He knew how easily Brooke could become so deeply entrenched in his heart that he'd never recover, because of how hard he'd had to work over the past two and a half years to not let that happen.

But if he was going to let her in, he wanted to be equally entrenched in her heart, too. But he didn't know how that was possible. Now that he'd seen firsthand what the other half of Brooke's life was like from their trip to Los Angeles, he knew he would never be able to compete for that spot. She was so far out of his league that he couldn't imagine ever being able to be everything to her.

Instead of pulling into the back parking lot of Back Porch Grill from First Street, like normal, he turned off Main Street at Center, so he could see the parking lot behind Best Dressed. Brooke's car was in its usual spot, Noemi's and Delbrina's next to it. He turned and drove to the parking lot behind the restaurant, parked, and looked in Brooke's direction when he stepped out of his car. He should take this chance to go talk to her before she left. Maybe all they needed was to talk.

He walked the block down Main Street and entered Best Dressed through the front door. Immediately he could hear the voices of Brooke and her employees having a conversation loud enough to make it to the front of the store, and it was obvious that none of them had heard the bell on the door. Maybe now was a bad time.

He was turning to leave, but he stopped when he heard Noemi say, "All because you didn't agree on what games to play at a ten-year-old's party."

"It's not about the party."

Cole took a few steps toward Brooke's offices, but halted, undecided whether he should stay or go.

"Well," Delbrina said, "it sounds to me like you're just running away from the problem instead of dealing with it."

"I'm not running away from a problem," Brooke said. "I'm running toward a bigger problem. I need to prioritize here."

Cole couldn't see any of them, but Brooke's voice got quieter and louder like she was moving from spot to spot and maybe bending down behind objects to pick up things. With the other sounds he was hearing, he figured she was probably preparing all the stuff she needed to take with her to New York.

"There are still so many things I need to do to prepare for my presentation with Van Zandt, and none of what is left has to be done here. Here, there are just too many things on my mind and too many distractions taking me away from what I need to do."

"Those 'distractions' are pretty important, too," Delbrina said.

Brooke must've set down something heavy because he heard a thump and a big exhale. "As my mom said, I don't have time for relationships right now—now's the time to work on the business."

"Brooke," Noemi said, "you've said it yourself a million times. People are important."

"They are. Which is one of the reasons I need to put all my focus into the By the Brooke label right now. Lake and Lane as a clothing line just failed. *Failed.* All because they let a relationship get in the way of the business. Do you know how many of their employees are going to be walking into work today and finding out that they're losing their jobs?

"This isn't just about me. So many people's livelihoods depend on me doing well. All of the people at my sewing manufacturing plant, my accountants, my graphics design people, my advertising and marketing people, my marketing reps, and the two of you. You all need paychecks.

"And that can only happen if I keep my eye on the prize and don't get distracted by a relationship that was probably doomed from the start."

All of what Brooke was saying had been shooting tiny daggers into him and his hopes for their relationship. But that last sentence stabbed a giant dagger right through his heart and he could no longer stand out of sight, waiting for their conversation to end so that he could talk to her. He walked to the opening between the front of the store and Brooke's offices.

"Doomed from the start?"

Brooke looked in his direction and her arms fell to her sides, her shoulders falling along with them. "Cole, I didn't mean—"

"No," he said, realizing the truth of what she'd said. What had he been thinking? He needed more stability in his life, and she needed more freedom. She needed someone who could hold his own in her world. Someone who was more naturally spontaneous. And probably a million other things he wasn't. "I think you're right."

Brooke fidgeted with the corners of a stack of papers on the design table beside her as she looked down, silent for a long time. "You're right," she whispered. "I can't give you what you need. Not now and maybe not ever."

She met his eyes just then, and Cole knew that the pain on her face was going to be burned into his memory forever. It was not the pain of somebody stressed about the load on her plate at the moment or of someone regretful of harsh words said; this was the pain of a final goodbye. Of not only a relationship ending but also a friendship. The pain of it nearly knocked him down. But he managed to look into those pained eyes of hers for a long moment before he acknowledged her silent goodbye with a nod, and then turned and left.

Ever since he'd fallen in love with Brooke two and a half years ago, he'd had a hard time imagining he'd ever get past her to be able to date someone else. Especially because they were such good friends and he saw her often. He'd considered moving several times, much more often at the beginning, because then he could both be away from the sadness of living in the same town as he had with his deceased wife and be away from Brooke. Then, maybe, he could someday start to fall for someone else.

But he and Sam had already moved out of the house that they had shared with Amanda. The only thing Sam had left of her mom was the restaurant and her grandma, and he always figured he owed it to Sam to stay.

But Amanda had been right. He also owed it to Sam—and to himself—to get remarried to someone he could give his whole heart to. Both of them needed someone in their life.

And finding out that the someone for him couldn't be Brooke was more than he could handle.

BROOKE

Brooke spent all weekend working on her proposal to offer custom dress designs for high-end customers for the part of her presentation where she had to show a new concept, as well as a lot of other last-minute items. And now that it was Monday morning, she had less than twenty-four hours before she would be presenting and it still didn't feel complete.

She worked on the balcony of her hotel. She worked at a table in an outdoor café in Times Square. She worked on a bench facing Conservatory Pond in Central Park. It didn't matter where she was, though—she was still every bit as distracted in New York by her relationship with Cole as she would've been back home.

And even in those few moments when she'd somehow managed to get distance from her thoughts of Cole, her body didn't forget. Her stomach had a constant dull ache of missing and longing and sadness at how things had turned out.

The truth was, she missed him. She missed the way they laughed together. She missed the way he smiled. She missed the way the space between his eyebrows would crunch together when he was looking down at his calendar. She missed the way he made her feel when he wrapped his arms around her. She missed all the ways that he showed love and concern for her. She missed that with him, for the first time in her life, she had experienced a romantic relationship that felt perfectly right. Meant to be.

Over and over again, she replayed that moment when she first realized that the way he looked at her—the way he had looked at her for years— wasn't just a look of friendship; it was a look of love. All this time and she had missed it.

And she missed their friendship. Every time she saw something funny or interesting, her hand automatically reached for her phone to take a picture and text it to him like she always did, and then she'd remember and miss his friendship all over again.

A few days before she and Cole broke up, Delbrina had told Brooke that she'd always had a hole in her heart and that all of her non-vital trips out of town had been her attempts to fill that hole. But all that was temporary, and in the end, it had left her plumb empty. She needed the kind of love that Cole was offering to truly fill it.

At the time, Brooke had blown off Delbrina's words. But now, as she was fully experiencing the pain of that empty hole, she knew that there was nothing that was going to fill it except Cole.

As she packed up her things and got into a pedicab to travel back to her hotel, her mom called to wish her good luck with her presentation the next day.

"Honey," her mom asked nervously, "you don't sound like yourself. Is your presentation not finished?"

She hadn't told her mom that she'd started dating Cole because she hadn't wanted to hear all the reasons why the timing was bad. And she hadn't wanted to hear all the reasons why a serious relationship was bad in general. She knew them all by heart already. But right now, she needed to talk to someone, so she told her everything.

"Oh, Brooke. I am so sorry, honey. Heartbreak is some of the hardest kinds of pain to endure. And I suspect that you're feeling the loss of your friendship just as exquisitely. If I could be in New York right now instead of Paris, I would wrap you in a tight hug and never let you go."

Brooke could face down impossible deadlines, harsh critiques of her designs in the press, or a panel of high-powered executives, but in having her mom's comfort over a failed relationship, she was suddenly thirteen again and her best friend was moving away and tears streamed down her face just as much.

Except for a few hitches, she managed to keep her breathing normal enough, but it took a while before she trusted herself to squeak out the words, "Thank you, Mom." She didn't fool the pedi-cab operator, though—he glanced back to see if she was okay, so she probably hadn't hidden her crying from her mom, either.

"That's what family is for, honey."

After a moment of getting herself together, she said, "Then why didn't you want that for me?"

"Didn't want what for you?"

"A family to lean on. I only have you and Dad. I've been raised on the belief that I don't need a man. But when you and Dad are gone, I will have nobody. Why didn't you ever want a family for me? I'm realizing how much family matters, and I don't think we're meant to be alone."

Her mom let out a long exhale and was quiet for a moment before she answered. "I think that sometimes, as parents, we try to shield our kids from experiencing the pain we experienced because of bad choices we made. And sometimes, regardless of our intentions, that shield ends up blocking them from experiencing some of the most wonderful things in life."

After a long pause, she added, "I'm sorry I never removed that shield for you."

"Thanks, Mom. But I'm beginning to realize that I had been holding onto that shield pretty fiercely myself, so maybe you couldn't have if you tried."

———

After she got back to her hotel, she washed her face and put her make-up on again, and vowed not to think of Cole again until after tonight's reception. She arrived at the swanky restaurant and was shown to the private room at the back, where a long banquet table was richly decorated in blues and silvers, Van Zandt's colors, and she joined the group of people who had already arrived and were mingling.

"Brooke," Ian said as she neared. "We meet once again on the opposite side of the country. Is this going to be a thing with us? Because I don't have any west coast trips planned anytime soon."

Brooke gave him a hug. "Good to see you, too. Maybe we can mix it up and meet somewhere in the middle next time."

"Lebanon, Kansas, here we come!"

Amica and Kale, the other two designers still in the running, joined them, and they swapped stories about how difficult the last three weeks had been.

"I had my first solo fashion show right in the middle of it," Ian said, and both Amica and Kale winced. "My assistant and I were literally finishing our prototype for our reaching-a-new-audience project right up until the moment I got in a cab to come to this."

"I was still making adjustments on the airplane," Amica said.

"Really?" Kale said. "I finished everything a week ago."

Brooke had just taken a sip of her drink and nearly choked. "You did not."

Kale laughed. "I so did not. But it was great to see your faces when you thought I had. I finished this afternoon."

"Me too," Brooke said.

The Van Zandt executives entered the room, and they mingled with the people they had last seen behind a long row of tables three weeks ago. Brooke's nerves were calming, and she found herself able to concentrate on the moment instead of having her mind elsewhere.

Then a couple entered the room that Brooke hadn't seen since she was ten. But she had been so entranced by the couple back then that she would recognize Arbor and Mazarine Van Zandt anywhere.

Everyone quieted and Mazarine said, "Welcome, everyone. Please find your seats.

The Van Zandts were at the head of the table and the four designers were in the seats on either side closest to them. The six people who had been on the panel of judges when they'd presented last time took the remaining seats. Brooke sat down in her seat, right next to Ian.

He leaned over and said, "Have you thought any more about the merger of our companies?"

"I have," Brooke said, "but I don't have a different answer for you."

All through the dinner, Brooke socialized with the other designers, the Van Zandt executives who were close enough to talk to, and the Van Zandts themselves. She had been her mom's plus one at a reception similar to this one once when they were welcoming her to the Van Zandt family after approving her cosmetics to go out in all of their stores. She had been impressed back then at how very different the Van Zandts' marriage had been from her own parents', and she had vowed then that one day she would have a marriage like theirs.

Somewhere along the way, she had forgotten all about that promise she'd made to herself twenty-two years earlier.

She found her mind going to Cole over and over, and every time it did, she forced herself to listen more intently or to ask a question of someone if the conversation had lagged.

After they finished their desserts, the Van Zandts stood up, holding hands, and thanked everyone for coming. "Designers," Mazarine said, "you will all be giving your presentations tomorrow, and soon after, one of you will have the distinct honor of not only joining the Van Zandt family but doing so as a featured designer. To those of you who don't gain that honor, I do hope you'll continue to submit proposals to us because we'd love to one day have each of you join us."

Arbor smiled at Mazarine and said, "This year we celebrate the thirty-sixth year of Van Zandt Department Store and our thirty-ninth year of marriage. We were told that both would fail by many, *many* people."

Mazarine chuckled and added, "Many."

"But I knew we wouldn't fail. I didn't worry about it for a second. Not only do we bring out the best in each other, but we both understood that marriage was a partnership, not a war. Whatever happened, good or bad, we were determined to face it together. And in doing so, we were able to accomplish so much more than either of us would've been able to do alone."

The words hit Brooke like a tidal wave crashing into her. This couple had entered into both kinds of partnerships that Brooke had spent her entire life being afraid of. Yet far from being doomed, they had flourished.

Mazarine looked at Arbor with such love in her eyes, even after thirty-nine years of marriage. Then she turned back to them. "In the dining room of our home, we have a proverb on our wall. It reads 'If you want to go fast, go alone. If you want to go far, go together.' Beyond question, we have gone far together, and we hope that, after tomorrow, one of you will go far together with us."

Brooke felt like she had been going fast her entire

career. Her entire life, actually. She always felt like she was in a race to learn more, to be more, to accomplish more. Listening to the Van Zandts had helped her to step back and take a look at her life from a distance. As she did, she realized that, although she'd been going fast, she was running in wide circles that weren't getting her to where she wanted to be.

And where she wanted to be wasn't just about where she wanted to be with her business. She discovered that it didn't matter how successful she made her business if her relationships with the people who truly mattered in her life failed. She did want to go far, in all aspects of her life. And as Mazarine said, she was only going to do that if she went together.

nineteen

COLE

Cole glanced out through the opening to where Samantha was working on her homework. She wasn't looking overly sad or distracted or unwilling to work. But she was missing her usual spark. The part of her that was most quintessentially Sam. He missed his Samster.

"Hiya, Boss," Hani said as he put on his apron.

Cole grunted. "You're late."

"Yeah, but I worked it out with Ann. That's cool, right, Boss?"

"Not if you don't run it through me."

Ann reached out and lightly touched Cole's upper arm with her fingertips. "Listen, I can stay for a while longer. Why don't you go out and grab some fresh air? You've been snapping at people all day."

Cole almost fired off a response about how he was just fine and didn't appreciate the commentary on his mood, but the fact that he wanted to give that response only made what she said all the more true. Instead, he gave a "Thanks, Ann," that came out more as a grunted mumble.

After taking off his apron, he headed out the back door and breathed the crisp mountain air in deeply. It was definitely a day for wearing a jacket, but the sun was shining and the cool air helped to calm his nerves as he breathed slowly in and out.

He glanced in the direction of the parking lot behind Best Dressed. He knew that Brooke was in New York and that her big presentation was tomorrow. Still, though, that knowledge didn't stop a part of him from wishing that she would show up unexpectedly like she tended to do. For any reason at all. Even to make him do something ridiculous, like race around his house, sing while he was cooking, or take an unplanned trip to get ice cream.

He realized that he *liked* that Brooke wasn't as scheduled as he was. It was too easy for him to fall into a trap of being too rigid, and she was the one who always pulled him out. Not until now, with it gone, did he realize how much he had appreciated that about her. How much he had needed it. How much he had wanted it.

Without realizing he was doing it, he found his phone in his hand, looking once again at the screen for a text from Brooke. Even before they started dating, he rarely went a day without getting texts from her. She had been gone a full three days already and hadn't texted once.

He shook his head. It was like he was having Brooke withdrawals.

He opened his photos app and touched a picture that Brooke had snapped when the three of them had been going to the booths at the Take Flight festival. They had gotten blue cotton candy, and in the selfie, he, Brooke, and Sam were all showing off their blue tongues, their faces shining with happiness.

He flipped through all his other pictures, most taken by Brooke, and then texted to him. Some pictures were just the two of them, and some were with Sam as well. Every single one of them had one commonality— happiness on their faces.

How could he have thrown something like that away?

But then he remembered the look on Brooke's face when he had stopped in Best Dressed last Friday morning. She hadn't wanted this relationship to continue.

He took one last deep breath and blew it out slowly. Ann had already stayed late for Hani, and he needed to get back inside so she could leave. Especially since she'd probably had a pretty long day already, having to deal with him being so irritable.

Back inside, he put on his apron, washed his hands, thanked Ann in a less gruff voice, and let her know she could go. He didn't know what Ann had said to Hani while he'd been outside, but the kid was working hard and barely saying a word outside of the necessities. Part of him felt bad and wanted to tell Hani that he could be his normal chatty self, but the bigger part desperately wanted the quiet.

Several times he found himself staring at the little dragon chef that Brooke had given him. Each time he shook his head, trying to clear it, and made himself get back to work.

When Susan came in to pick up Sam, Cole wiped off his hands and went up front to greet her. As usual, he thanked her for coming to get Sam, then hugged Sam and told her when he'd be by to pick her up from her grandma's.

As the two of them were about to leave, Susan said, "Sam, do you mind waiting for me by the door?"

Sam nodded and went and sat on one of the benches in the waiting area.

Susan studied Cole for a long moment, and he tried hard to smooth his face into something less like an ogre. Susan exhaled, her face softening. "Amanda wouldn't have wanted you living in a state like this. She wanted you to be happy and to move forward."

"I know she would. It's just...complicated."

Susan nodded. "I know." She paused for a long moment, then added, "For what it's worth, Amanda would've approved of Brooke."

An emotion-filled breath escaped Cole. He hadn't realized how badly he'd needed to hear those words until they came out of Susan's mouth.

———

An hour and a half later when Cole showed up at Susan's house, Sam opened the door and he was surprised to see that her spark had returned.

"Daddy, Daddy," Sam said, "come see what I did!"

She grabbed hold of his hand and pulled him into his mother-in-law's kitchen and then held out both arms toward the papers, signs, and little cars made out of colored, folded cardstock that filled the dining table.

Sam picked up one of the cars and held it toward him, resting on both outstretched palms. "Remember when we made this? I took it to school and Anna said it was so cool and told me that she would pay me a dollar if I made her one too. A whole dollar!

"And I still had two of the cardstocks that had the car template on them, so I made one for Anna. When I colored it yesterday, I was trying to decide which colors and almost did it the colors *I* wanted it to be. But then I got thinking about how Brooke said that she puts herself in the other person's shoes and tries to imagine what they most want, so I did that. When I gave it to Anna today, she said it was the most beautiful coloring job she's ever seen! And then she paid me the dollar."

She set down the car and picked up another one. "Lincoln and Jayce saw and said they wanted one too. So Grandma took me to Elsmore's today and I used that dollar from Anna to make more copies of the cars, and I colored this one for Lincoln. What do you think?"

Cole smiled at his daughter. "I think you did an amazing job and he's going to love it."

"Well, I figured when other people see Jayce's and Lincoln's cars, they're going to want to buy one, too. So then I decided that it is time for me to become a businesswoman too. Come see— I made this order form where people can say how many cars they want, and if they want to choose a color or have me choose for them. And I made these flyers to pass out to everyone to advertise, just in case Jayce and Lincoln and Anna talking about them isn't quite enough."

As he marveled at his daughter and everything she had created, it hit him how much Sam had learned over the years from Brooke's example. Sam told him all about her big plans and big ideas as he helped her to get everything packed up to take home. Then he thanked Sam's grandma for supporting her project.

All during the drive home and while they were eating the chicken fettuccini Alfredo and salad that he had brought home for dinner, Sam kept telling more about her plans, her excitement not dying down.

"And I figured that if everyone in my class goes crazy for these and this business goes well at school, then maybe I can make some to sell at a booth in Snowdrift Springs during the summer. But if everyone doesn't," she tapped a finger on her temple, "I already have ideas in here for my next business."

Every time Brooke went out of town, Cole had seen it as Sam being deprived of someone in her life who she really cared about. But he was realizing that having a successful businesswoman like Brooke in Sam's life instead was providing her with a role model who was helping her to grow into a strong, capable, confident person.

"You're thinking about Brooke."

His eyes flew to Samantha, who was sitting with her elbows on the table, her chin resting in her palms.

"I can tell because you always get hearts in your eyes when you do."

"I do not."

"Don't worry; they aren't like cartoon hearts that are big and red. They're like...shiny sparkly hearts, and you have to look close to see them."

"So I've been walking around everywhere, showing my sparkly heart eyes to everyone, and I didn't even know it?"

Sam nodded. "Pretty much." A smile spread across her

face. "Also, you just admitted that you think about Brooke, like, non-stop."

He laughed. That much was true. He wasn't sure she'd been far from his mind for more than a few seconds for a while now.

"Do you miss her?"

He nodded. He missed everything about her.

He had always thought that he wanted someone who was a homebody like him. Stability was important to him, and he felt like he couldn't get that from Brooke. It wasn't until now that he realized that the kind of stability he truly wanted was stability in love itself, and over their almost three years of friendship, Brooke had been showing that all along.

Sam stood up and took both of their plates to the sink. "When I'm sad and missing Mom, you have me talk about her and that always makes me feel better. Do you want to talk about Brooke?"

He shook his head. He didn't want to burden his daughter with his scattered thoughts and relationship woes.

She walked back to the table and put one hand on each of his cheeks, turning his face to hers, her eyes fixed on his with all the determination an almost ten-year-old could muster. "Daddy. You're the one who told me not to keep my feelings trapped inside me."

He stood up and walked around the kitchen, hands on

his hips, trying to decide what kinds of things he could share with Sam that would show that he practiced what he preached, without putting too much on her. His mind was a jumbled mess of thoughts, memories, realizations, hopes, and fears that he wasn't sure he could even pull into sentences.

"Brooke and I are opposites. I like everything scheduled and she likes to make plans at the last second. I like being at home and she likes traveling the world. I'm a single dad and she said she wanted to always be single. But even with all that, I guess I'm just realizing that maybe we aren't as opposite as I thought. Maybe we're not opposite at all in the things that matter."

"Like what?"

"Like caring about people and doing what we can to help them. Working hard. Having fun. Loving you. Loving each other."

Sam grinned and clasped her hands together in front of her heart. "You love her! I *knew* it!"

He paused and then nodded. He'd never admitted it out loud before but it was something he had known for a very long time.

"I have to find a way to make things right with her." He paced through his small kitchen some more. "I have to convince her to give us another shot. I know the two of us can make it work. Do you think she'll want to try?"

"Daddy. She has hearts in her eyes, too. I've seen them."

"You have?"

Sam nodded.

He wished Brooke was in town right now. He'd race to her and tell her how he felt and somehow get her to change her mind about long-term relationships. Specifically, a long-term relationship with him.

"You need to tell her you love her, Daddy."

"I know, but she's still in New York. I don't want to tell her over the phone."

"So go to New York!"

"I can't. I've got to take care of you, and I can't leave the restaurant with so little notice." He knew all of this. Still, though, his mind raced through ways to make it work. Through what it would be like to go to Brooke in New York and confess everything to her.

"You help people all the time, Dad."

He looked at his daughter.

"Let them help you back."

He stopped pacing, eyes on Sam. "Do you really think I can make this work?"

"Yes. You should go drive to Denver, get on a plane, and fly to New York. When you get there, you should go up to her building holding a dozen roses in each hand and yell 'I love you, Brooke McClellan!' loud enough that all of New

York can hear you. And then she'll come down and she'll put kisses all over your face, *mwah, mwah, mwah*. And then all the people in the streets will say, 'Aww!' and they'll have hearts in their eyes just from watching you and Brooke, and then you can both fly back home holding hands."

Cole smiled at Sam, shaking his head. "You paint a pretty convincing picture there, Samster."

So convincing, he had to find a way to make it work.

BROOKE

T he energy in the green room at Van Zandt was one of nervous anticipation. All four designers— Brooke, Ian, Amica, and Kale— were dressed in suits and pacing, shaking out their hands and mumbling to themselves as they went over their presentations.

"Distract me," Ian said to Brooke. "Since I'm going first, I won't have time for these nerves to relax on their own and I'm going to go in there a frayed mess. Please. Distract me."

Brooke motioned to the suit hanging from a hook on the wall. "The suit you made for your 'branching out' requirement is brilliant and amazing."

A genuine, relaxed smile crossed Ian's face. "Not every girl wants to wear a fancy dress to prom. If she wants to wear a suit, she should have one that's every bit as fancy as one of your dresses. I think this might be my favorite thing I've ever designed. But that's not going to work, Brooke. Step it up. Distract me with something other than my presentation."

The thing that was distracting Brooke was thoughts of Cole, and how she could possibly change some things in her life to make herself available for the kind of relationship he had been offering. The more distance she got from what she'd had within grasp, the more she realized that what she could have with him was something beautiful and priceless and worthwhile and exactly everything she never knew she wanted.

She didn't want to talk about him before her presentation, though, for fear that it would leave her scatterbrained and unfocused. Or possibly emotional, which would be disastrous. So she looked all around the room, grasping for anything else to bring up to Ian.

"I've got it," Ian said. "Let's talk about combining our businesses into a partnership.

Brooke laughed. "I'm shocked that we've been in this room for a full thirty minutes and you haven't brought it up yet."

"Okay, now hear me out. I know the statistics, Brooke, and your dad isn't wrong—partnerships are the business type that fail the most frequently. Usually, that's because both partners don't have similar visions, morals, or work ethics. But partnerships can also be the most successful business type. This," he said, motioning at all of Van Zandt, "is one of the businesses where a partnership was successful."

Over the past several days, Brooke had been realizing just how many things she'd been wrong about. Things she'd grown up her entire life believing. The awareness that she could be wrong about this, too, opened her mind to hearing his proposal more than she ever had before.

Ian faced her, excitement filling his eyes and his voice. "Brooke, we graduated from the same design program together. We started our businesses as babies at the same time. We have practically grown up together as fashion designers and business owners. We've known each other long enough to know that we have the same work ethic, the same goals, and the same vision. The fact that we've been at this for the same amount of time, and the net worth of both our businesses are virtually equal, proves that."

He paused a moment, then his words came out more relaxed but more earnest. "I know that your dad says that equal partnerships never work. But Brooke, I think that being so equal is exactly why this partnership *will* work."

An assistant opened the door and stepped into the room. "Ian Bancroft, you're up in two."

Ian nodded his acknowledgment at the man and then turned back to Brooke. "So say we partner and everything works, because it *will* work. We'll have a company with more contacts, more resources, double the brilliant brains powering it, double the workforce, and when one of us is working a deadline and a trip out of town needs to happen, we'll have double the people who can do it."

"Sir," the assistant said, "it's time. Would you like me to help you with your things?"

"Yes. Just give me one moment." He turned back to Brooke. "What do you think?"

"I think," Brooke said, drawing out the words as she worked through so many things in her mind, "that you might not be wrong. This could be good for both of us. I will definitely think about it more."

A grin spread across Ian's face. As he headed toward his portfolio and suit, he turned, calling back, "This is going to be good. I know it."

"Good luck with your presentation," Brooke said.

"Thanks," Ian said, pausing at the door, smiling wide. "And thank you for so fully distracting me from my nerves."

The Brooke who stood in this room last time, as one of a group of twelve of the thirty-six original designers, would've never guessed that Ian's words could've made so much sense. The old Brooke would've closed off her mind to the possibility of a partnership working before Ian even said two words about it because she had known partnerships were doomed since she was old enough to know what one was.

But she stood in this same room today, as one of four designers, with the knowledge that not everything she had known and believed in the past was absolute. She had been pulled toward both Cole and Sam from the start, not realizing how much she had been wanting a husband, a daughter, and a family, right from the very beginning.

And how much she wanted that family to take the spot of highest importance in her life.

———

Brooke chatted with Ian, Amica, and Kale after each had their turn to present and came back to the green room, each collapsing onto a sofa in relief at being done. Then the assistant popped his head in and told Brooke that she was up.

Brooke walked into the presentation room with the same panel of executives sitting behind the same long row of tables, but this time both Arbor and Mazarine Van Zandt were seated at the tables too.

This time there was no question about what she should prepare— Van Zandt Corporate had given all of them a very specific list, and she and her team had dedicated their all in the previous three weeks to perfecting the items on that list. Presenting was one of her strengths, and she walked in confident that she was going to nail it.

Brooke greeted each of the executives as she entered the room, then placed her oversized lookbook on the easel at the front and placed a regular-sized copy in front of each of them. She started by showing off all the designs she'd like Van Zandt to consider carrying, then talked about all the places where her product could currently be found, then moved on to explain the details about her manufacturing center, their current output, and what their maximum output was.

As she was giving each part of her presentation, everything clicked into place—partnering with Ian's label would be like two halves of a whole that would be more effective together than either two would be apart.

Brooke presented her conceptualized plan to design high-end, unique, and customized dresses to fit the individual personalities of customers needing special dresses for big occasions. Then she showed off the dress that she had designed for Sam, smiling at the positive comments from the panel. They asked her several questions— all ones she had the answers to— until the timer sounded the end of her presentation and she thanked them for their time.

When she headed back into the hall with her portfolio and Sam's dress, she was shocked at the realization that she didn't want to go to the lunch Van Zandt had set up for the designers where they could talk shop to their hearts' content. She didn't want to hang out in the green room after that, even though she loved being with people who had the same passion as her.

And the biggest surprise of all was that she didn't want to go to the party tonight that was planned for the designers in town, along with all of her friends who were designers living in New York.

All she wanted to do was to go home. She missed Cole terribly and just wanted to go see him and find some way to not only repair the damage done from the last two times she'd seen him but to figure out how to stay together as a couple.

For the first time since she was a little girl, she allowed herself to picture what it would be like to have Cole as a husband. To have him to come home to at the end of each day— a partner to share her life and her hopes and her dreams and her struggles and her disappointments with. And to not only have Cole as a husband but to have Sam as a daughter. A family to come home to.

The thought made her feel so complete that she inhaled a quick breath and leaned against the wall in the hallway, eyes closed, relishing the feeling.

Noemi had been right when she'd talked about Cole being the only one who could fill the hole in her heart. Because right now, the mere thought of being his partner in life seemed to fill it to the top.

And right along with it, all the non-essential trips she usually took to network with other designers, with visits to boutiques thrown in to legitimize the trip— visits that could just as easily be done by her very capable marketing reps— no longer felt vital.

At times in her life, when thoughts of a long-term relationship flitted into her mind, she had always squashed that thought by telling herself that her responsibility to the relationship would hamper her ability to go on business trips. Or any other kind of trip. That thought always suffocated her.

It hadn't occurred to her that a fulfilling relationship might just make her desire to be away from the ones she loved simply disappear.

There were definitely trips that *were* vital to her business, and those still drew her in, and she knew they likely always would. And as the designer and CEO of By the Brooke, there were business trips that only she would be effective in taking. Those trips excited her.

But trips vital to her business but not necessarily ones she needed to take personally did come up at inconvenient times occasionally, like when she was struggling to meet a deadline. If she wanted a family, she knew things would come up that she'd want to be present for. If she had a business partner, they could cover for each other on those kinds of trips as needed.

A single breath of a laugh escaped her. The Brooke from three weeks ago never would've considered having a business partner or a husband, and now she was realizing that the one might make the other all the more sweet. Partnering with Ian might allow her to be able to have more time to spend with the people she loved the most. And that was what really mattered.

She walked back into the green room and Kale, Amica, and Ian all looked up at her, giving smiles of camaraderie at having all survived the presentation at the end of the shared three-week race. Amica scooted over, giving her space on the couch between her and Ian.

Brooke held up a finger and said, "I've got to do one thing first. Ian?"

Ian must've been able to tell that there was more in her expression than relief at having finished, like it had been with Kale and Amica, because he stood up, a hopeful question on his face.

She held out her hand. "Before I sit, I'd like to shake the hand of my future business partner."

Instead of shaking her hand, Ian grabbed both of her hands. "Are you kidding me right now?" When she shook her head no, he jumped up and down holding her hands, just like Delbrina and Noemi had when Van Zandt had named them a finalist, and she laughed, his contagious excitement filling her.

———

Back in the green room after their lunch, the four of them waited as first Amica and then Kale were called back in to meet with the panelists for final questions. When the assistant poked his head in a third time, he announced that they wanted to see Ian and Brooke together. They both gave each other questioning glances, then followed the assistant back to the presentation room and stood before the panel.

Mazarine thanked them for coming back in, and then said, "Ian mentioned that you two might be merging your businesses. We would like to know what you think the possibility of this might be, because it may affect our decision."

Brooke's eyes flashed to Ian's.

He gave her a sheepish shrug. "I didn't mean to spill the beans. In the question and answer portion, it just kind of came out. In my defense, I was fresh off the excitement of you saying you were considering it less than two minutes before I walked in here."

The panelists chuckled.

"So is it true?" one of the executives asked.

"It is." Brooke hadn't even thought of the fact that it might affect their decision and hoped it wouldn't mean that it would reflect negatively on their scores, or worse, that it would mean disqualification.

Mazarine nodded her head in acceptance, a smile on her face. "May I give some advice?"

"Please," Brooke said. If anyone could use advice in facing two potential partnerships—one in business and one in love and life— it was her.

"Identify what each other's strengths and weaknesses are," Mazarine said, "and don't ignore the more hidden strengths. Your combined strengths are the things that are going to make your business stronger together. And above all else, support one another. Never forget that their success is your success."

Mazarine stood up and walked around the tables to shake both of their hands. She smiled. "I wish a long, happy partnership for you both."

Brooke walked out of the room floating with the knowledge that this partnership with Ian was going to make possible an even more exciting and rewarding partnership with Cole. If it wasn't too late to convince him that she was ready to put their relationship first.

twenty-one

COLE

Cole paced in the lobby of Van Zandt Corporate Offices in downtown New York City, palms sweaty, nerves frayed. The plane ride had been stressful. He hadn't had to fly often in his life, and this was the first time he had ever flown anywhere alone. Once he had landed, it had been a race to get everything ready before Brooke's meetings were supposed to end.

The nervousness had been a constant companion for the past twenty-one hours as he had hastily gotten last-minute plane tickets, coordinated with everyone at Back Porch Grill to take over his duties while he was gone, worked things out with the mom of one of Sam's friends to take Sam to and from school and let her play at their house until Susan could pick her up, asked Susan if Sam could sleep over at her house, and worked through plans of how to let Brooke know that she was exactly perfect and that he loved everything about her.

He'd known the entire time they'd been friends that she never wanted to get married, but he would take having her in his life in any way she was willing.

And now he stood in this massively high-ceilinged lobby, facing the open stairs that Brooke would be walking down when she was finished. Three hundred red balloons were spread throughout the spacious lobby in groups of three or four, at all different heights.

He hoped that when Brooke came down the stairs and saw them all, she'd have the same look of wonder and happiness as the girl had in her childhood favorite book and that she would know without a doubt that she was loved.

There was an extra layer of pressure added as more and more Van Zandt employees made their way down to the lobby every few minutes. Most acted like they needed to be in the lobby for some reason just then and were doing their best to act busy but angling themselves so they could watch the stairs, too.

Cole wiped his hands on his pants again. Finally, he heard voices from the stairs just before Brooke rounded the upper flight of stairs that were blocked from his view and turned on the landing to face the lobby and descend the second half of the stairs.

Brooke and Ian, the designer he'd met at the fashion

show in L.A., along with another man and a woman, all froze as they saw the lobby.

After a minuscule pause, Brooke's hands flew to her mouth and her eyes flashed across the people in the lobby until they fell on him.

She stood at the top of the flight of stairs wearing a black suit, a bright blue shirt, and heels, looking unbelievably amazing. The hands over her mouth and the distance hid her expression. He wasn't sure how she was going to respond, and fear seized him.

Then she dropped her arms, one hand finding the railing, and walked down the stairs as the other three people remained at the top. Cole didn't take his eyes off her as he moved forward in the path he'd left in the middle of the balloons, warmth and nerves and happiness and fear warring inside him during the last few steps to meet Brooke at the base of the stairs.

"You remembered about the red balloon." Brooke grabbed both of his hands in hers. "I can't believe you remembered."

Cole rubbed his thumb along hers. "I don't think there's much I've forgotten about you in the past two years and ten months. I still remember what you were wearing the day you walked into the restaurant for the first time."

As she searched his face, he could feel the eyes of a

couple of dozen people on them, all holding their breath, waiting to see what would happen next.

"Brooke, we've been friends for a long time, and I've been in love with you for almost as long. The longer I know you, the more amazing I realize that you are. I can't offer you all the glitz and glamour of the fashion world, but I can offer you my whole heart." He paused a moment, then added, "And good food."

He wanted to also offer her a ring and a promise to be hers for the rest of their lives, but he knew that wasn't an option. That was okay. The smile that lit up her face was enough.

"Cole," Brooke said, and he could hear the hesitation in her voice.

"I just want us to continue dating," Cole said. "If it never turns into anything more than that, it's okay."

"So, Cole Iverson, you're saying that you've loved me for more than two years and you never told me?"

He chuckled and moved his hands to her back. "Say you'll keep dating me, and you'll know I love you 'when I hold you in my arms all snug and tight and tell you that I love you every night.'"

———

Sam ran up to Cole and Brooke where they stood watching the action, hand-in-hand. "I can't believe the day of the party finally got here!" Then just as quickly as she'd run up to them, she ran back to where all twenty dukes and duchesses were dressed up in their finery and trying to keep a couple of dozen balloons up in the air using their wands.

Cole laughed. "I think that's about the ninety-seventh time today that she's run up to me and said that. Thank you for convincing me that it was a better idea to involve her in everything instead of making the party a surprise."

"I think she had a lot of fun planning it," Brooke said. "And I was so impressed at how long this many kids sat around the tables making their wands. That was a pretty good idea, too."

Cole nodded. "And they definitely needed an action-packed game when they were done."

Everything had come together even better than Cole had imagined. Bo Charleston had offered to have a couple of his horses pulling a flatbed trailer bring all the kids to the party. Eli Treanor had used some of his props from Team Up to make the trailer look like a royal carriage, and Brooke and Sam had put sparkly unicorn horns on the horses so they'd look like the unicorns that pulled the carriage in the book.

Brooke and Sam had decorated his normally empty extra room to make it fit for royalty, and when the dukes and duchesses arrived, they all entered the party through the tower slide that Nate had built.

The ten-layer cake that Cole made— just like the one

in the book— turned out pretty fantastic, if he did say so himself. The parents of all the kids and all the other adults who had come to help seemed to be loving the foods he'd crafted on the dessert table because their chatting groups never moved far from it.

Brooke kissed his cheek. "I'm going to go check on the music for the sleeping spells dance."

Cole nodded, and he watched her walk away until she disappeared into the back corner. After looking down at the schedule on his phone, he held up two fingers to let Sam know that it was almost time for the next thing they had planned. She gave him a nod in acknowledgment.

When the alarm on his phone went off, Sam ran around to the backside of the tower slide, got in the little cubby, and flipped the switch. The platform raised her up and turned her to face the room and the microphone she'd been using to emcee the event.

She stood in the princess dress Brooke had designed, watching the dukes and duchesses play for a small moment before she called out, "Annnnnnnnd, stop!" Her heavy breathing from the tiring activity sounded through the microphone as she held it close to her mouth, waiting as all the balloons fell to the floor. "Okay, now everyone use your wands and push those balloons off to the side over there. A little bit further. Perfect! Okay now come back; I've got to tell you what we've got coming up."

Once all the kids were gathered again in front of the

tower, Sam said, "We've got a photo booth set up over there with some royal props so we can all get pictures of being fancy, then while everyone is finishing, we're going to play a game called Sleeping Spell Dance. You guys are going to love this. When the music is playing fast, everyone needs to dance all crazily. But when it stops, it puts a sleeping spell on you and you have to fall to the floor asleep until it starts again. Got it? Good. Wait! Come back, Riley and Janet. I didn't say it was time yet."

Cole chuckled. He hoped that his daughter never lost that confidence.

"Because we have one other thing happening before the photo booth. Parents and helpers, you need to come over here for this, too. Come on, come on. Over here."

Cole's brow crinkled and he pulled up the party schedule on his phone. After the balloon activity was the photo booth. There wasn't anything else in between. And the only other thing on the schedule besides that and the dance was eating the refreshments. He looked up at Sam, confused. She wasn't looking his way, though— she was still directing the adults to where she wanted them to stand.

"Brooke," Sam said through the microphone from her perch on top of the tower, "will you turn on the soft music, please? Nate, will you turn the sparkly lights on the tower and dim the other lights?"

Once both were done, Sam grinned one of her biggest

grins. "This is the part of the party that I'm most excited for than anything else. I'm not even kidding, everybody, it's even more exciting than the tower slide or the unicorns or the cake. I didn't even think it was going to happen, and then when I found out that it would, I begged and begged and begged can it *please* be part of the party."

Cole's eyes found Susan in the crowd. Did Samantha plan an extra activity with her while he had been in New York? Susan met his glance but just smiled and looked back up at Sam.

Sam held up *Princess Samantha's Perfect Party.* "Remember when I read this book in class during Book Share? Well, I didn't read the ending then, so I'm going to read it now."

She opened it up clumsily with the microphone in one hand and then made a show of clearing her throat. "Princess Samantha's Perfect Party was such a big wish, though, that it was too big for just one magical helper, so Princess Samantha actually got two—a fairy godmother and a fairy godfather."

Cole smiled when he realized she was making up a new ending to the story as she went along.

"And the dukes and duchesses and all the subjects and especially Princess Samantha were delighted when they found out that the fairy godfather and the fairy godmother had fallen in true love with each other!"

Cole might have blushed a little. He looked around the room for Brooke to see what she thought of Sam's impromptu storytelling, but the tower lights only lit up the people gathered in front of it. The rest of the room was cast in shadow and he couldn't see her at all.

"At first, the fairy godmother tried to keep it a secret that they were in love. But then she decided that she was sooooo in love with the fairy godfather that she wanted to spend forever with him, and she wanted everyone to know it."

Sam motioned with her hand to the middle of the crowd and whispered into the microphone, "Now I need you guys to all split apart a little bit. Make a path."

Once the crowd separated into two halves, Sam said, "But most of all, the fairy godmother wanted the fairy godfather to know it."

Brooke made her way through the opening everyone had cleared and came up to where he stood near the base of the slide, looking uncharacteristically nervous.

"Brooke?" He wasn't exactly sure what was going on and hoped she was going to fill him in.

She smiled at him, relaxing. "Cole," she said. "You've been my best friend—" She glanced out at Whitney in the crowd, standing next to Eli, and with a breathy laugh, amended it, "my best *manly* friend for a long time. Long enough that I've been able to see, firsthand, your strength of character.

"And more than long enough to know that I like who I am best when I'm around you. You're the person who has most helped me to see that I had been completely wrong about partnerships. I wasn't being insincere when I said that you are my very favorite thing about Nestled Hollow. I love you, Cole. I want to be more than friends with you. Always."

Cole searched Brooke's eyes, finding the truth in the words she was saying.

"Cole Iverson, will you marry me?"

The crowd let out a collective gasp, and Cole was sure his was in there, too. "You want to get married? For real? You, Brooke McClellan, want to marry me?"

"I mean, I can't offer you the most skilled help in the kitchen, but I can offer you my heart." She paused, then added, "And surprise breaks in your schedule. So what do you say?"

Cole wrapped his arms around her and they both turned around in circles, happiness escaping as laughter as he did. Her face looked just as happy and flushed and glowed in the golden lights from the tower.

He reached out with his knuckles and ran them lightly from her temple, down her cheek, across her jaw, and stopping at her chin. He brushed his thumb back and forth on her lips. "I'd say that it takes an incredibly accomplished businesswoman to be able to make an offer this impossible to turn down. Yes, Brooke. From the moment you first walked through that door so long ago, I had hoped we would one day get to 'yes.'"

She put her hands on his shoulders before she slid them up to his neck and he pulled her in close. After a glance at her lips, he closed the gap and pressed his lips to hers.

Their kiss on the bridge had held a sense of urgency like the chance had been fleeting and would disappear at any moment. As Brooke's lips moved against his this time, slightly parted, the kiss felt more sure. Confident. Like the beginning of something that wouldn't ever end.

"Everybody," Sam said through the microphone, "this is the part where you cheer! If you're wearing a hat, throw it up into the air! Throw the balloons up into the air!"

Cole's kiss turned into a smile against Brooke's lips as balloons fell on them from all around. "I do believe the entire kingdom showed up to celebrate our engagement."

Sam sighed a happy sigh into the microphone and switched to her book-reading voice. "And everyone found out that the fairy godmother and the fairy godfather were going to be King and Queen, and they and Princess Samantha and all the kingdom were going to live happily ever after. The end."

Brooke tickled her fingers into the hair at the back of his neck, sending chills down his back. Her face was still barely an inch from his. "So what's the proper protocol here? Do we bow to our gracious guests?"

He smiled and nodded, then they both turned to the crowd of their friends and Sam's friends and, holding hands, took a bow. Then Cole leaned Brooke back in a dip. "Here's to 'happily ever after,'" he said, and then gave her another kiss.

BROOKE

Brooke turned off the freeway onto the Nestled Hollow exit, her headlights spilling onto her hometown. She had been gone a full five days and it had felt like forever.

It had only taken Van Zandt a week to announce By the Brooke and Bancroft Limited as joint winners—apparently hearing that they were going to merge their companies made their decision so much easier than choosing one of the four companies separately.

Between all the work to get Ian's suits and her dresses ready for their catalog and all the manufacturing to get the items ready to go out in all stores, and all the paperwork, planning, organizing, and strategizing it took to merge two companies, the past six months had been the busiest of Brooke's life. Saying yes to two mergers within three days

— one to merge her company and one to merge her life with Cole's— had been ambitious.

After winding her way through town, Brooke parked in front of the Holt's home, then turned off her car and got out, stopping to grab a blanket out of her trunk. Then in the light of the stars and a sliver of a moon, she snuck next door to Cole's yard. Once she was on his property, she spread the blanket on the grass and sent him a text.

> Brooke: I just got a text from Mrs. Holt. She says there's a bear in your yard that you should probably scare off.

She glanced at the clock— 10:47. That meant he was already done reading; hopefully that didn't mean that he was already asleep. It had barely been long enough for him to have been able to send an answer text before the front door flew open and Cole stood in the light of his front porch, wearing a t-shirt and pajama bottoms, squinting out into the darkness.

"Brooke? Are you really here?"

She stepped into the light and he leaped off the porch, skipping the steps entirely, and wrapped her in a hug.

"It seems you missed me as much as I missed you."

He brushed his knuckles down her temple. "How did you get back so soon? I thought it was going to be another two days."

"The lawyers and bankers decided we had finally

crossed the last *T* and dotted the last *I*." She shrugged. "It's possible they were as sick of the minutia as we were."

"So you and Ian officially have a parent company now?"

Brooke nodded and slid her arms behind Cole's neck, slipping her fingers into his hair. "And the names *By the Brooke* and *Bancroft Limited* as brands are still intact. My dad will be so proud. The moment the suits told us we were free, I pulled out my phone and booked a flight."

"No victory celebration with your new business partner?"

"We decided we wanted to get together sometime soon and celebrate when we've got our fiancés with us."

His eyebrows shot up. "Ian got engaged?"

"Last weekend. He was still ecstatic when I arrived." She motioned to the blanket she'd spread on the ground. "So, my soon-to-be husband, would you care to look up at the stars with me? I missed them, too, while I was in New York."

Cole lay on his back on the blanket, his hands under his head. Brooke snuggled up next to him, her head on his shoulder, looking up at the millions of stars spread out in every direction across the Nestled Hollow sky.

"I should warn you," Cole said, "Sam has been working on a card to give you when you got back in town."

"That's so sweet," Brooke said. Then after a pause, added, "Why do I feel like there's more to the story?"

"Because the card says something to the effect of, 'I

love you. I missed you. I really want a baby brother or sister. I just thought you should know.'"

Brooke laughed a deep, loud laugh that came straight from her stomach. "Tell her to give us two months to officially tie the knot, and then we'll get right on that."

Cole flipped to his side so he was facing her. "Wait, really? You're serious?"

"I am," she said and drank in the smile that spread across Cole's face at her words. "It just feels exactly right."

"It really does."

"Besides," Brooke said, "the mental image of you holding our little baby is irresistible."

"Over and over, you just keep finding ways to make me the happiest man alive."

Brooke traced her fingertips across his cheekbone. "I love you," she whispered, then she leaned forward and pressed her lips against his, knowing to her core that everything about saying yes to marrying this man was exactly, perfectly right.

———

Author's note:

I hope you enjoyed reading Brooke's and Cole's story as much as I enjoyed writing it!

I'm excited for you to read the next book in the Nestled Hollow series! It's Tory's and Nate's story. Tory owns Love a Latte, and when a tree falls on her building during a lightning storm, doing extensive damage, Nate steps in to help her rebuild. You can pick up *Love Again at the Heart of Main Street* here.

Do you like audiobooks? I am putting more and more of my audiobooks on my YouTube channel every month. Subscribe so you'll be notified each time one releases.

—Meg

Read next:

Get your copy

Her life is too chaotic for love. But adding more chaos is exactly what brings him—and love—in.

Tory is living her dream running her own coffee shop, Love a Latte, and raising four young kids. But her divorce left her doing it all on her own and not always succeeding. She'd consider marrying again someday— as long as the man was the complete opposite of her ex. But she really has no hope of that, because who would ever willingly step into her chaotic life?

Not only has Nate's marriage failed, but during the entire time he was married, he'd failed at convincing his ex that they should start a family. His lack of a love life can't be helped, but with his busy construction company and crew, he can help others plenty.

When a tree falls on Love a Latte during a lightning storm, causing extensive damage to the building, Nate steps in to help Tory rebuild. As the damaged building is being mended, can working side-by-side also mend their damaged hearts?

The feel-good sweet romance you've been hoping for. Grab your copy here.

get the series

Coming Home to the Top of Main Street

Second Chance on the Corner of Main Street

Christmas at the End of Main Street

More than Friends in the Middle of Main Street

Love Again at the Heart of Main Street

More than Enemies on the Bridge of Main Street

Meg Easton is the *USA Today* bestselling author of contemporary romances and romantic comedies with fun, memorable, swoon-worthy characters, and settings you'll want to pack up and move to. She lives at the foot of a mountain with her name on it (or at least one letter of her name) in Utah. She loves gardening, bike riding, baking, swimming before the sun rises, and spending time with her husband and three kids.

She can be found online at www.megeaston.com

Sign up to receive her newsletter and stay up to date with new releases, get exclusive bonus content, and more.

If you liked this book please leave a review. Your review can help other readers find books they might fall in love with.

youtube.com/@megeastonauthor
bookbub.com/authors/meg-easton
instagram.com/megeaston_author
facebook.com/MegEastonBooks
tiktok.com/@megeaston_author

9 781956 871159